RUN

"Gillian Zane created a short but smoking hot and intensely scary story that is only just the beginning." - Seeing Night Reviews

FIGHT

"I am hooked on this series and can't stop reading them..." - Dana ~ The Dirty Smut'atter

LIVE

"There's action, revenge, love and sex with two very hot men. What more could a girl ask for?" - Romance Between The Sheets

JUSTICE

"Gillian has created a world we've all feared in our deepest darkest dreams, she paints a picture so vivid it comes to life in your mind. Each scene seemingly more real, more intense than the next. Emotions running on high, fueled by adrenaline, hunger, fear. What will you do when the world as we know it comes to an end?" - Carrie Renteria

A PARAJUNKEE PUBLISHING BOOK

Cover Design by Parajunkee Design

Editing by Raw Books Editing Services

www.romance.rocks

gillianzane@gmail.com

::: created in the USA :::

JUSTICE

NOLA ZOMBIE

BOOK FOUR

To my T.I., TSGT Bradley, your hat made
a lasting impression.

JUSTICE

NOLA ZOMBIE

SERIES by GILLIAN ZANE

PARAJUNKEE
DESIGN
& PUBLISHING

"*Beware that,* WHEN FIGHTING **MONSTERS**, you yourself do not *become a* MONSTER... **GAZE** *for when you* LONG INTO THE ABYSS. THE **ABYSS** *gazes also into you.*"

- *Friedrich Nietzsche*

ONE

KNOW STUFF ABOUT STUFF

REBEL

I felt alive when I was killing *them*. It was horrendous to think this, but my only moments of clarity were when I was off base and on the hunt. The only moments when the burden of my new life wasn't at the fore-front of my thoughts. When I was at the home base I felt like I couldn't breathe, always looking over my shoulder in a perpetual game of cat and mouse. Here, the enemy was real. I could spot the enemy. I could kill the enemy. There was nothing to think about, there was only one constant.

The enemy wanted to eat me. The enemy must die.

It came for me with its mouth chomping in a macabre parody of chewing. It looked like a toddler begging to be fed. This was no toddler though; it was an adult male, overweight and dressed in the remnants of a suit. His clothing hung from him, ripped to shreds, dried blood cling-ing to every square inch of him. His belly was exposed, the grey skin of his large gut jiggled in the night air as he extended his arms as if to give me a hug.

Even though the suit was ripped and stained, it was obvious it was expensive. The ripped lining had designer written all over it. Before the world ended, I was in the market for my first suit, to land my first real job. This guy could have been my boss or maybe a client one day. Not anymore. Those days were long gone.

Leather was more practical than Italian wool anyway.

There were a lot of polo shirt and suit encased biters in this area of New Orleans. Lakeview was one of the most prized and over-priced areas of the city of New Orleans. Before the world ended, of course. It was now my home. Also known as the hole I crawled into.

I had a 70124 zip code, something I didn't think would ever happen in my lifetime. A bunch of rich, workaholic snobs had lived here. They were all a bunch of dead rich snobs now, caught unaware trying to get their last bit of work done while the world went to Hell around them. They were cursed with wearing the same designer suit for eternity, or until I took them out.

This one had lost his shoe somewhere and one of his arms looked like it was about to fall off. Half of its face was chewed on, its cheek bones were exposed, viscous strips of flesh hung from its eye socket like garish decorations. Its eyes were locked on me in hunger.

It crossed my mind to let it eat me, maybe I could trip and all it would take was one bite. The brother fighting at my side, my fellow Southern Clansmen wouldn't let me turn. He'd put a bullet in my head quicker than you could say "after-life." It wouldn't be that much pain, a quick bright light, and then I would be done with this place. I would be done with this messed up world.

"Rebel, what the fuck is your problem?" Bear called from the other side of the street. He was wrestling with his own biter.

I planted my knife deep into the head of the rotting corpse in front of me and it fell to the ground at my feet.

A citizen was cleaning up the mess as we took out each biter. He was dressed in a full-body hazmat suit that we had found with the rest of the Army gear that came with our newly acquired base. He ran over to me and grabbed the biter I had killed and tried to pull it by the arm, but its arm came off, so he had to grab it by the chest. He pulled it toward the lawn by the lapels of that fancy suit. He tried to throw it onto a stack of the other dead, but the biter was too heavy. He pushed him close to the bodies as best as he could. From what I could tell, there were no other biters on their way. We were done for the night. Time to light the fire.

We had been killing biters for the last four hours. I was dressed in leather, for easy clean-up, but I was still covered in gore. The biters leaked, it was nasty. When you stabbed them, black blood burst out of them and sprayed you. They also had this bizarre tendency to liquify which also tended to splatter. Good thing I was single, I could barely stand myself.

Four hours of biter killing was a new record. We had a technique. Bear had found an old boom box, the kind that didn't need a phone or Mp3 player to work, and we had found a CD of AC/DC. We cranked that music up and it was like calling pigs to be slaughtered. It was my idea of course, and I have to say, it was a great one. I was tired of getting surprised by the biters every time I went on patrol. They would pop up and be all *grrr* in your face and if you weren't paying attention, you were pushing up daisies.

About two weeks ago I shared my idea with Senior, the president of the Southern Clan Motorcycle Club and dictator of our newly formed Apocalypse Party; he waved me off and told me to do whatever the hell I wanted. That was the best thing he had ever told me. If it wasn't about drugs or women, he couldn't care less. It's why I liked being out here, away from them, away from my "brothers" and the drugs, the women, and the stink of excess. It was real out here. In there, it was akin to a bomb ready to explode and I didn't want to be around when the timer went to zero.

"Where's your head at, dick sucker?" Bear strode over to me. His nickname was true to form, he was fat, big and hairy, a monster of a man. He had been that way for as long as I could remember.

"He wasn't going to get me. I was looking at him. They're falling apart, in a year they might be skeletons. You think they'll decompose until they're nothing?"

"Now, that'll be fucked up, a skeleton running after you. Is that possible?"

"I didn't think a walking, biting corpse was possible," I shrugged.

"No, you know what I mean, the bones, they need shit to hold them together, right? Like muscle and fat and stuff. You're the college kid, you study that shit? Would they be able to walk around as just bones?"

College to the Southern Clan bikers meant you knew about everything. If there was a question, call in Rebel, he went to college. When I told them I didn't study that particular topic, they looked at me stupidly, like what did that matter? I went to college, I should know stuff about stuff.

"Yeah, you need muscle to keep the bones together." I closed my eyes and clenched my fists, only opening them when I had taken a few deep breaths. I had learned this trick a long time ago, long enough to make it not so obvious that I was pissed or annoyed. I was a legacy Southern Clan member, meaning my father was a NOLA SCMC, his father before him was a founding NOLA SCMC. When I was thirteen, my dad gave me my first tattoo. It was the Southern Clan's Confederate Flag, I had no choice. I was a man and I had to show my manliness with a tattoo, the rest of the ink would come when I got full membership and my colors. Afterwards, he got one of the club girls to take my virginity. She thought it was cute when I told her she didn't have to, that she could lie and I would tell everyone we had sex, So she gave me head, insisted on "popping my cherry," her words, not mine, and told everyone I was the best lay she'd had in a long time. This didn't go over well with the club, though. Everyone knew she had screwed the president's son a few days earlier, who had also just turned thirteen, her words put a target on my back and it's never been removed. She didn't realize what she was doing. Or at least I hoped she didn't. It was another day in the life of a Southern Clan member.

The citizen was done with his biter stack. The dead made a neat pile of decomposed flesh that stood five feet tall. He doused the pile of corpses in lighter fluid and then threw a match on top of it. The biters went up in smoke. They burned easily for some reason and usually only left a pile of dust and a few scattered bones in their wake.

"I'm gonna bring the citizens back. I'll relieve you in six hours," Bear said. We were at the lookout location on one of the main drags in the neighborhood we had taken over. We had three lookout locations and Bear and I rotated shifts with one other brother for the location on Canal Boulevard. It was boring work, but we had to stay alert, you never knew what could happen in this world.

I nodded and made for the big house we used for watch. It was a raised two-story monstrosity that had housed some lawyer and his family before the biters took over. I climbed the stairs and set up shop in a second floor bedroom, the big window at the front had a good view of the street. It was going to be another long night.

I hated the monotony of being on lookout, but I hated being back at home base even more. I wanted to be out there doing something. Not sitting here waiting for that something to happen.

My mind drifted to thoughts of escape. I wanted to get on my hog and get the hell out of the area. They wouldn't chase me down. My dad probably couldn't care less if I lived or died. I would be on my own though and this world wasn't a place to be on your own. Someone always had to have an eye open. There were biters everywhere and if it wasn't biters, it was other humans. The humans were worse.

This had been my routine lately. I was stuck in a perpetual loop of thinking to leave and then talking myself into staying. I hated it here, but I was as good as dead if I went off on my own. No matter where my macabre thoughts led me earlier, I didn't want to die. Living meant staying with the club until something better came along. Hopefully I would last until that better showed up.

TWO

TINY BULLSHIT

REBEL

After four boring hours of staring at the street and hoping for a random biter to give me something to do, Tiny, one of the enforcers, came tearing down the street on his hog. We had taken to only using the bikes in an emergency since they were so loud and tended to draw the biters to us in droves. We didn't want to lead them to our base, so bikes were on lockdown. Ironic, since we were a motorcycle club. I spotted him as soon as he turned onto Canal. I could tell it was Tiny because he was the only one that wore a bright red dome, what the MC called their helmets.

I went outside to meet him. If he was driving by, he would wave me off. He didn't drive by. He pulled up onto the lawn, but didn't cut the engine. The big bike rumbled and the sound was reassuring, even though Tiny looked panicked.

"Senior's bitch killed him tonight, gutted him like a pig. She took out Fatz and Parrish on the way out. You gotta return to church, man, the whole place is a shitstorm. I'm rounding everyone up."

"Wait, what? Senior's dead?" I asked.

"You ain't listening, man. He's a total rotter. We found him bled out on the floor, she didn't even have the decency to put one through his brain. She probably wanted to take more of us out if he would have turned, the cunt, get your shit and head back. It's crazy town over there."

"Well, damn," I grumbled.

If I was processing this correctly, Senior had been taken out by the girl he had recently claimed as property. From what I remembered she was new, a recent acquisition from some rednecks out of Slidell, a city to the east of New Orleans. I wasn't allowed to hang out in the main area of the base that much, what we called church, since I wasn't the most popular of the brothers, but I had seen her a few times, sitting next to Senior, or dancing for the men. She was striking, I remembered that much, enough to make me do a double take. She was also young, early twenties at the most. It had made me sick to see the bruises on her face and body, most likely from Senior. If she took out Senior, things were going to get interesting, real fast. I had no love for the man. Being gutted by the girl he kept as property was almost poetic justice. But I wasn't excited to see Junior, his son, step up to the plate as president.

Senior was a sadistic and cold man, but his son was pure evil. There was no better way to describe it. I had grown up with Junior and I was well-versed in his darkness. My father was Senior's Sergeant at Arms, had been since I was a kid. Brandon Junior and I were the same age so we were always together, along with two other legacy kids, Jazz and Eagle. Junior and I never liked each other. Tolerated was a better way to describe our relationship. I wasn't looking forward to Junior's rule. I might have to put more thought into disappearing on lookout one night. I had been toying with it for a long time. There was nothing holding me back now. In fact, I might have no other choice. Death loomed before me if I went at it alone, but death was pretty much a guarantee if Junior was in charge. Tolerance as kids had led to hatred as adults. He kept himself in check because of our fathers, but there was no one to keep him in check now.

Tiny tore off into the night, rounding up the other lookouts, telling them the news, I assumed. I grabbed the mountain bike that I had stashed in the back of the house and rode the ten blocks to Robert E. Lee Boulevard where our base was located. My club had taken over the strip mall that ran along Robert. E. Lee Boulevard and West End Boulevard in Lakeview. It had started as a refugee camp run by the National Guard, but Senior, the now former president, didn't like their rules, so he had taken over the place.

My father told me Senior ran the soldiers off, but I didn't believe him. The National Guard wouldn't run off, but knowing Senior and his ways, he would have killed them. Their bodies were probably a burn pile now. The same fate that awaited me. The handle bars wobbled in my hands.

Should I go now? Make a break for it?

The streets were dark. It was probably the best time to do it. I heard the unmistakable moan of a biter in the distance. I had nothing on me, I was out of ammo and I didn't have any of my stored food. I kept the bike headed toward base. I could always leave another day.

THREE

DRILL SERGEANT BABY

BABY

I never wanted to be a fucking drill instructor. Never had the patience. Never had the fortitude. You break the worms down, then you've got to bring them back up and put them back together in working order. I was good at breaking people down. The bringing them back up part was what stumped me.

That sounds terrible, even in my own fucking head.

I never claimed to be a nice person, but I did try–sometimes. I was good at tearing people down, but I wasn't some bitch that enjoyed sadistic mind games. I didn't enjoy making people cry like babies, I had a knack for it. There was something about me that really pissed people off. It was something about the way I talked. Something about the way I held myself. *Shit, it was mostly about how I looked.* And that really pissed me off.

The way I looked was a curse.

I didn't like being self-conscious about my looks. That was for sorority girls and aging housewives, not for girls like me. But I realized real fast in life that cuteness would be the bane of my existence.

It wasn't my fault that I was barely five feet. It wasn't my fault that my voice was a bit squeaky or that I was a natural blonde and I was sporting a bigger rack than most chicks twice my size. It wasn't my fault that people consistently underestimated me. They treated me like a dumb child and then got pissed when I showed them their ass.

At first, I got angry about the pixie jokes, the Police Academy references, the stupid nicknames and the constant sexual harassment. Now I used it as fuel. I haven't figured out how to inspire that kind of thing in others. *Some got it, most didn't.* You either break life or let it break you.

The cool thing about a post-Z world, the victims have all been eaten.

It took spine and a little bit of luck to make it in this world. You couldn't sit around and lament about how the world dealt you a bad hand– 'cause we're all in the same boat.

We're all fucked.

There were some things I couldn't shake, though, in this new shithole of a world. Like my current nickname. I guess I should be grateful that they had nicknamed me Baby instead of Sergeant Hooks, or G.I. Barbie? I couldn't sit back and love all over it, though. Being constantly referred to as a demeaning term of endearment wasn't good for my self-esteem. It pissed me off every time it slipped out of someone's mouth. And it was happening more and more as people at this damn compound became comfortable with me.

Apparently, I wasn't scary anymore.

At first when someone called me Baby to my face, I punched them. It was a lot of punching. I've had to reign it in a bit, counting to ten usually worked. Alexis, who was ranking up there as an actual friend, who happened to be female, something new for me, was trying to break me of my distaste of the name. She was doing this by constantly using it. And since I felt guilty about punching her, I was stuck with it.

Alexis, who everyone called Lex, came to the Compound right after Z hit. She came with Blake Miller and Zach James, my bosses, and she's turned this place upside down ever since. She is the exact opposite of me as far as looks with bronze skin, dark hair and eyes, and almost a foot taller- no one would call Lex cute. Stunning, maybe, not cute. Not like me, who people liked to pat on the head and speak to in little girl voices. I usually responded to this with something bitchy, but it never goes over well.   I might not enjoy being a bitch, but Lex did. It was her most likable trait, in my humble opinion. When she turned her bitchiness on me, I didn't like it much, though. Especially when she used that damn nickname.

My retaliation was making her do lots and lots of push-ups. Payback's a bitch.

"Ya fucking killing me, Baby," she whined from a prone position at my feet.

One. Two. Three.

"Talk shit again, and you get fifty more," I hollered in my deepest, butch, drill instructor voice. I might not have planned on being a drill sergeant, but it did relieve a bit of stress.

My drill sergeant back in the day, Staff Sergeant Kilpatrick, had been a walking, talking psycho. She had made my boot camp experience utter hell. Taking a special liking to me, she had made a point to constantly single me out. I never quite knew why her attention always fell my way. It might have been my uncanny ability to see the humor in most situations and remark on it. I remember the hat she wore with wicked clarity.

She could get the brim of the hat right on the bridge of my nose and tear me a new asshole with remarkable usage of the English language. All while leaving a fine sheeting of spit over my face.

I wish I had a hat. I wouldn't have been able to reach Alexis' nose though, I was too short. *Bummer.*

I hadn't given Staff Sergeant Kilpatrick much thought in the last five years, but she seemed to be resurfacing a lot lately since I found myself using some of her techniques. Zach James had assigned me ten survivors with the express instructions to "get their shit together." They were a mixed lot, a few were self-trained, like Alexis, having learned quick and fast in this new world we lived in. Others were complete newbs, having somehow made it this far with little defense training. But they were eager and listened to me, and that was all I could ask for. They knew what we were doing was probably going to save their asses, so they paid attention. Well, most of them. Lex was a bit of a smartass and gave me shit every time she could. It's why I liked her.

The new world we lived in wasn't friendly, it wasn't kind. In a little under a year, humans had gone from the top of the food chain to the bottom. We were choice, Grade A, prime meat and death waited for us around every corner. To make matters worse, even the other survivors couldn't be trusted. It was every man for himself in this shithole of an apocalypse and my group of survivors planned on being on the winning team.

This is where this bit of boot camp recreation came in. Gotta get the civvies in ship-shape order. Or whatever those damn Marines called it. I wasn't hip on seaman slang. What it came down to was one thing– these civilians had to be turned into soldiers in a few weeks' time. It was do or die, we had no room for error. If you stepped one foot out of our compound, you were fighting for your life, so they had to learn to fight.

To achieve this I was running drills with them, interspersed with a lot of cardio, followed with weapons training and then close-combat techniques. The goal was to form quick reaction skills, urban warfare skills and close combat defense moves. All of this would help them against our everyday enemy- the dead that walked the streets. The zombies that had brought the world to its knees last year. It would also help them with the mission our group was planning. A mission not against the dead, but against the living, specifically a group that had taken over an area of New Orleans called Lakeview.

When Z hit, most people had grouped together to survive. My group was comprised of my former co-workers and people we had picked up along the way. We were uniquely prepared for the end of the world, being conveniently employed as mercenaries. Most of us were former special forces, and my bosses were in possession of a self-sufficient compound in the middle of the swamp on the outskirts of New Orleans. Our bosses were well-prepared, surprising for two Marines.

I give them a lot of flak for their branch, but they did have their heads on straight. They had put this place together quickly and now we were surviving, trying to carve out a new existence. We had a rather good leg to stand on, at least compared to others.

The problem with our cushy existence and our adherence to a logical way of life was that we had become the only order in the area. Here we were trying to lay down some kind of moral and logical existence for ourselves, a fact that helped us as a group to survive, and it basically put a target on our backs.

Not all the humans left in this chaotic world were like us. Some were desperate, starving or a bit off their rockers, watching the world collapse around them. Others were using the end of the world to set up sick, depraved kingdoms. We were either an obstacle or potential victims.

The group we were targeting in Lakeview fell under the latter description. Depraved was putting it lightly. At first we had been content with leaving them to their side of the city. Lakeview was twenty miles away and in this world that was like being across the country. We had tried a no engagement policy until they had stepped over their line.

We couldn't ignore them any longer. We had gotten a look at what was going on within their ranks, what they were doing and how horrendous it was. It was bad.

Three of the women doing pushups at my feet had suffered at the abuse of these men. The men who had declared Lakeview their domain. The women had been held captive, abused and forced to witness and participate in numerous unspeakable acts. I had only gotten part of the story, but what I had heard was bone-chilling.

My life wasn't a Norman Rockwell. I had been through some nasty shit in my day, especially when I landed in foster care, but what the men in that gang were doing made my life seem peachy. I had only heard pieces and parts from Lani and Lex, but it was nasty. Repeated rapes, forced drug use, keeping the children hostage to control the parents, not to mention the constant abuse. It had me chomping to get in there and kick some ass. The human population might be severely in decline...but we could deal with losing a few more.

"Stop!" I yelled to my group and they all fell to their chests on the ground, some panting. Alexis was at my feet. She rolled onto her back and grinned up at me maniacally. I glared at her and she laughed at me.

"I'm not scared of you anymore," she panted. I could have kicked her.

But I also wanted to smile. The fact that she was laying on her back at all was fantastic. Only a week ago she would flinch when you touched her anywhere near her injured skin. It must be nearly healed now. Thinking of her back had me itching to kill someone.

Alexis hadn't told me the whole story. She had mentioned a few key points to establish the Lakeview group's patterns and behaviors. But I had a clear picture of how she had made it out of there. I had been right there to witness her escape. She had been covered in blood, barefoot and beaten badly. Her back had been a mess of cuts and bruises from a beating she had endured. She could hardly hold herself up but managed to take down two of the gang members, and their leader.

Bleeding, broken and barely standing, Lex had helped another female, Melinda, to escape–and she had even gotten Clara out. Clara whose murderous intentions had gotten them both captured to begin with. Everyone wanted to see Clara pay for her crimes, but no one could quite figure out what to do with her since killing her was a little too much for the majority. Clara was currently locked in the infirmary. She traded one prison for another. I didn't feel bad for her.

I didn't want to think of Clara right now, it only got my blood boiling. Time for a change of scenery.

"Everyone up on their feet, stop whining. Time for some close quarters tactical training." I clapped by hands for emphasis, like an asshole. Like Kilpatrick used to do. It was all about the motivation. I set a quick pace, running in an easy trot as they got to their feet. Once they caught up, I waved them on to the secondary warehouse we had on the compound. Zach and Blake had converted the mostly unused warehouse into a training facility. We had put up some temporary walls and set up a few sleeping berths like the women had described were constructed in Lakeview.

We didn't want any surprises and we wanted to be as prepared as possible. The group in Lakeview was a biker gang that had taken over a temporary military installment that was being used as a refugee camp. The gang went in and killed the soldiers who were left in the camp and took over as the leaders. The camp was in what were once a grocery store and the adjoining stores in a strip mall. It would be cramped quarters for fighting, dark because they had no electricity, and the bikers would be at an advantage since they were familiar with their surroundings.

It was going to be nasty.

A close quarters fight would be almost inevitable and I had to prepare these survivors for one of the most horrendous forms of combat. It's one thing to shoot a target from far away and watch them drop. It's another to be engaged in hand-to-hand combat, or shoot someone within close range. Nothing like seeing a person's head explode and getting the gooey spray back.

In our briefings we had decided it would be best to draw most of them out of the buildings, but we knew we wouldn't get them all out. Some would most likely stay behind to guard their stockpiles and the women. This would force us to go in and drag their stinking asses out by their stupid leather vests. It wouldn't be fun since they were armed to the teeth from what we would could tell.

"I think we've about had it with target shooting. You're all competent with a weapon and you can shoot a target. But the thing about these bikers is they aren't going to hold still and let you shoot them." I pointed at Lani and handed her one of the trainer guns. It was bright orange and looked like a toy, but it had the same weight and grip as a .38.

"We've covered how to clear a room, movement, stances and now we're going to put it all together with our weapons. If we go into the store to get these douchebags out, we'll be in tight range, and there won't be time to get in a perfect shooter's stance. Best case scenario, we'll catch them unaware and we'll be able to flush them out of the store and on the defensive. Worst case, we'll have to go in and fight. If that happens, we'll have to use some critical tactics that none of you are ready for. These bikers will be within five feet of you, coming at you and most of them are handy in a fight. Barroom brawl style, at the least, military trained at worst. Across the room you have time to get off a few rounds, if you miss, you shoot again. Close range, you barely have time to get your gun in place. Come around the corner and I'm right here waiting for you." I directed Lani and she did as told, holding her gun to her chest with both hands and swinging around the corner.

I came at her fast and she punched out with the gun to open fire, but I was too quick for her. Before she could extend her arm in a shooter position, I had swatted the gun out of her hand and taken her to the ground.

"Dammit," she cursed, her eyes brimming with tears. Lani was young, she had turned nineteen and Z had hit right after she graduated high school. She was also a perfectionist. Every mistake she made caused her to get emotional. It was annoying, but I respected how hard she tried.

"It's okay, this got me too the first time." I stuck my hand out and she accepted the help up.

"In a close quarters gunfight you have to implement tactics that you aren't used to and you can't use both hands with your weapon. Most of you are used to gripping it with two hands and being able to spread your legs. When only a few feet from your attacker, you need to be able to block and attack. This means you need one hand free. Keep the gun close to your chest, cock it to the side slightly so it doesn't catch on your clothing when you fire, but keep it tight so you can aim properly. You don't have to extend your arm. Extending your arm gives you better stability, but you don't need that in close quarters. Your attacker is right in front of you." I maneuvered Lani into position, showing her how to hold her hand. She nodded that she understood when I looked at her questioningly.

"Keep this in mind if you have a gun pointed at you- they have that arm stuck out in your face, and all it takes-" I made a quick motion with my hand to demonstrate a disarming technique.

"Pair off. I want one to practice with the tight attack and the other to try and disarm." I clapped my hands and they obediently paired up. I dispensed a cup of water from the cooler and chugged it back, surveying my group. They were doing well. I was surprised with some of them, Lani in particular and the female that had come out of Lakeview with Alexis, Melinda. Doc had wanted her in the infirmary with him, since she was a trained nurse, but she was intent on helping us take down Lakeview, which I respected.

They were the only girls in my training group. The rest of the gang was comprised of the men that had come with Blake Miller, from Houston and had only been a part of our compound for a few months. Liam, Bret, Ray and Orlando were all competent fighters but still a bit green. I also had some of our original survivors in my group. They weren't former employees, but have been with our group since right after Z hit, Justin Crisp, Jimmy Camp and Duke Nunez were all competent fighters, now. I saw Alexis had paired up with Duke, which I was grateful for, he wasn't the sharpest tool in the shed and he was a misogynist so I wanted to see her put him on his ass a few times. Duke was good to have in a fight because he was big and rather strong, but his crude humor and inappropriate behaviors grated on my nerves. Plus, he was cocky, the kind of cocky only dumb people can achieve. My stupidity tolerance was low.

The door of the warehouse slammed opened and Blake Miller walked through them. Blake had recently shaved off all his pretty hair since hygiene had taken a bit of a downturn lately. We were working on formulating the perfect soap recipe, but right now we had to rely on goods that were scavenged. We still had plenty of soaps and shampoos, but our supplies were finite. Long hair was a vanity in a world that didn't do well with material needs. Most of the women that kept their hair long only did so because they could tie it up or pull it back in a ponytail for easy care. It would take a bit more "end of the worldness" to set in before us females were shaving our heads. The men were comfortable with that look, not the women. Give me a few months without shampoo and maybe a lice infestation, and I might give the high and tight look a try. I shivered thinking about it, I liked my locks.

Blake was a tall man, so of course, I had to look up to him when he stood next to me. He had been one of my bosses before Z hit and now he had taken a leadership role at our compound. We called it S-Island for Survivor Island, and Blake Miller, his partner Zach James and Alexis were kind of the de facto ruling class. Not by any right or vote, just because it's how it happened. Blake and Zach because they owned the island our compound was located on and had supplied us with the weapons, food and shelter that we used, and Alexis–well, because she was their girlfriend. Both, yeah, she was a more tolerant girl than me.

I had only worked for Zach and Blake for a short while before the world ended, but they made good decisions and I trusted them. In the middle of the shit, that was worth more than gold. And Alexis was a natural leader and she kept the boys' heads on straight. Plus, she listened to me. I would follow all three of them to Hell and back. I had no problem with their leadership.

"We're going to scavenge Trivox tomorrow and then leave for Lakeview the following day," Blake said after a quick greeting. "I want your final say on who stays and goes from this group by this afternoon. And I'm serious, Hannah, if you don't think one of them could survive a one-on-one with one of those Lakeview pervs, they stay back. I don't want to lose anyone." I nodded and looked over to the group. The only two I could honestly say would be an asset in this fight was Alexis and Duke, which grated, I wasn't a fan of Duke. Duke Nuñez was a civilian and hadn't integrated well with the rest of the team. He was lewd, lacking in hygiene and thought the way to a girl's heart was by being a total stalker. He was strong though, and knew his way around a weapon. He might not be my favorite, but he would be handy in a fight.

The rest of the team I was giving about an eighty percent chance of survival, Justin and Lani were my bottom two. Justin wasn't aggressive and had a tendency to panic, Lani was still weak from her ordeal. She hadn't eaten properly in six months and was so young. I told Blake my thoughts and he nodded.

"Both of them will fight me if I try to get them to sit out," I sighed. "Lani wants payback, Justin wants to prove that he's worth a damn. I don't think they'll be an issue, but I don't want to see them go inside," I said quietly so I wouldn't be overheard.

"You're right. We'll keep them off the frontline. They'll have to be content with bringing up the rear. You did good here, Hannah, seriously, your training will save their lives." He patted me on the back and then walked over to Alexis, who tried to ignore him as she was ordering Duke on his knees and zip-tying his hands like we had practiced.

We had this. Lakeview was going down.

FOUR

REBEL BABYSITTER

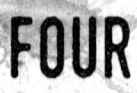

There was no one guarding the door. It stood cracked open to the elements and anything that might wander in. I walked into our main building without any resistance. This was a really bad sign. I yanked on the door, forcing it to slide open and walked into chaos, even though I wanted to turn and run.

The brothers were talking loudly, milling about, nothing but a sea of black leather and our colors of red, white and orange.

Junior was by his father's office and was yelling at the top of his lungs. "You bunch of incompetent pricks!"

He was standing on the counter that ran around the glass office Senior had used for his living quarters. The counter had been the customer service area for the grocery store, but it was now a bar, or a place to do drugs. It was usually littered with ashtrays, meth and bottles of booze.

There was nothing up there now though, but Junior. It was completely clear and bottles were strewn across the floor, broken, with the smell of alcohol pungent and noxious permeating the air. He was in a real tirade.

There were no females around. Even the one they called the "house bitch" was tucked away in the back where they kept the girls. I'm sure some of the Old Ladies were hovering near the back of the room, hidden, but listening. It was their usual MO. The brothers' wives were not allowed to mingle with the men, or speak out, or leave the base. They were kept in a different area than the property girls, but still locked up. Their only status as an old lady kept them from being traded, or from another brother requesting a night with them.

I tried to stay in the background. I didn't want to be seen or noticed. Our group consisted of forty members and they were all gathered in this room. It would be easy to stay to the back and remain unseen.

"How did she get a knife? How did she get out?" Junior ranted from his perch. I noticed my father motion for him to lean down, and Junior squatted, allowing him to say something in his ear. My father was obviously trying to explain what had happened or make some excuse for what went down without the others hearing him.

"I knew that slut was no good!" Junior finally puffed out, like he knew, like he had seen it coming. He stood up and looked down at us from his lofty view on the counter. He was still young, my age, barely twenty-three, but he wore the road on his face, his eyes already lined with crow's feet. His hair was a dark shock of black on tanned skin, hinting at an ethnic heritage, though he insisted it was the Cajun in him. He was tall and well-muscled, which made him strong and tough to beat in a fight. As a teen he had taken me down twice, until I got smart and started taking mixed martial arts in my spare time. He never took me down again, *by himself.*

"My father is dead. It looks like I'm President now, brothers," he called down to us in his deep voice. A low murmuring went over the crowd of men and then a steady stream of clapping and a few catcalls. "My father Brandon Senior is now gone, but not forgotten, and I'm ready to lead the

Southern Clan!" More catcalls and cheers.

"We've got a new world here, a new world with no rules, with no heat breathing down our necks. We are truly free, my brothers!" His raised his arms as if preaching on a pulpit and looked down at us with a grim smile on his face.

"With Senior's death it will be hard, but we can do this. We'll have a new focus, a new goal. We don't have to slink around in the shadows anymore. No more running from the law and living off the dregs of society. We were always outlaws, but now in this world, with no government, no pigs, the outlaws will rule! We make the rules now, we are in charge!" The room erupted in cheers and I clapped along, in case anyone was paying attention.

I suddenly felt sick to my stomach. *Was this how it felt to be a German in the 30s?* I looked around at my brothers who were all eating this shit up. They looked almost gleeful. Only a few had grim looks on their faces. I didn't know if it was because they were mourning Senior or because of what Junior was saying.

"I'm appointing Mick as my Vice President, and Eagle as my Sergeant at Arms," he said and there were a few gasps from the crowd. My father had been Sergeant at Arms for a long time, it was expected he would stay in his position when Junior took over.

"Shouldn't we take a vote?" someone called. I craned my neck to see who it was, but they were staying low.

"This ain't a democracy. My place, my rules. We doing things differently now and until things get straight, I don't want to hear shit from y'all. You don't like it, you can walk." He jumped off the counter into the crowd and restless murmuring went over the group of bikers, glee turned quickly into doubt. We usually had a vote, there was always a vote. The president had the final say, but he listened to his brothers. Junior had other things in mind though.

"Bayou, get Senior's body out of here, we're gonna have to give him an old school Viking send-off tonight, and get one of the old ladies to clean out his room," he said to one of the brothers standing near him. Bayou had been licking Junior's boots for years. He hurried off like a typical lackey.

"We gonna have one hell of party tonight, brothers, send the old bastard off with a bang," he finished and turned around, motioning for Eagle to follow him and they went into Junior's living area.

I had a really bad feeling about how things were going to change under Junior's leadership.

I could understand Senior's motivations as a leader. They were always centered on self-gratification. He was an addict, I could understand addicts. I couldn't trust them, but I knew what his motivations were. Junior was motivated by something entirely different and I didn't understand it. He was a mean bastard and a lot of his decisions were made from cruelty. He was also greedy and power hungry so there was no telling what he could do to the club. Sometimes power could motivate a person to act for the good of the group, a solid foundation gave a person more power, so building up the group would benefit a leader.

Junior was smart, which was a scary combination with his other traits. His smarts might also help him keep our group together. If he kept his head straight he could get us pointed in the right direction. Again logic and misguided hope was giving me another reason to stick around. Maybe Junior would turn things around.

I knew the hope stemmed from the fact that I didn't want to be on my own. I didn't want to leave and face this world as a lone wolf. My mind cooked up a million reasons Junior might be a better leader than his father. But deep down inside I knew it was time to go. Even if Junior turned the group on the right path, he still hated me. I would never feel comfortable around my brothers with him as the leader. I would never be accepted. It was either exist on the fringe, or leave.

I went to my sleeping berth. I wasn't allowed to bunk in the main area where the weapons and the women were stored. I had lost that privilege when I refused to dish out a beating to a civilian who was caught taking more food than his daily allowance.

My berth was in the secondary living area in the former coffee shop next to the main building. They had knocked down a wall, and it was a crumbling mess of sheetrock and hanging electrical wires. They used the kitchen in the former coffee shop as the food prep area. The nasty thing about it though, was that the connecting wall was from the bathrooms in the grocery store. Between the bathrooms, now abandoned because of the lack of running water, and the smell of the old food, it was a nasty area. I didn't know what was worse, the smell of old piss or rotted food. My sleeping area wasn't prime real estate that was for sure.

Looking around the ten by ten area I called my personal space, it was rather pathetic. A few sheets strung up between walls and a window. I didn't have much to my name. I had my weapons, which I was still allowed to carry as long as I had my colors on. I kept my weapons on me at all times, my .357 nestled in my belt and my .22 in my boot. I also had a machete attached to a loop that I had fashioned on my belt and I let that hang at my hip and kept it close at hand when I slept. In my berth I had a few books that I didn't want to part with, a couple pictures of my friends from college and the MREs, Meals Ready to Eat, I had been stashing for the last couple of months. I kept those hidden under a blanket and fashioned as a side-table, as if it was a crate that I kept things on. We weren't allowed to hoard food.

I removed the few items I kept next to my bed and pulled the blanket off of my stores and added an MRE to my growing collection.

When out on patrol each brother was given two MREs for every twenty-four hour patrol period. I had made a habit of only eating one of the MREs in that timeframe since their high calorie count could sustain me for the day. I also had been stashing canned goods I found in houses, along with other items in different areas around the neighborhood. I was required to turn in any food that I found, and in exchange I was given a "food credit" from the club. These food credits, or creds as they were called, could be cashed in at any point for extra food, females, alcohol, drugs or weapons.

For each patrol and watch I completed I was given creds, but the perk of doing the dangerous, off-base work was that you got to take food with you. This translated to a lot of food creds. I wasn't going to pay for sex and I abstained from liquor and drugs which would inhibit me, which left weapons. I hadn't amassed enough creds for a new piece, but I was getting there. The downside of amassing a lot of creds was that it became pretty obvious I wasn't spending them and the brothers had become suspicious. They didn't understand why I wouldn't take a girl or a hit.

I tried blending in better after I noticed the suspicious looks. In the last month I came up with a plan. I was using my food creds on girls, one girl in particular. I would act like part of the group, even if it went against all my principals. It was too little, too late, though. My unwillingness to indulge was obvious to the others and it painted me as an outsider.

A throat cleared behind me and I threw my blanket hastily down on top of my stores and turned quickly to face whoever was behind me.

It was Jazz, who's probably the only brother I trusted in the club. But it wasn't by much. Jazz was in Junior's inner circle, a place I could have been also, if I had learned to play the game better. I was never good at politics, or keeping my mouth shut.

"Your girl was the one that escaped," he said with no preamble.

"I thought it was Senior's property, the Hispanic chick," I said casually and I slipped my hands in the pockets of my jeans to hide that they were shaking from almost being caught with the food.

"Three got out. Senior's bitch, your girl, and the other new one that came in with Senior's property. Those three were the only ones that got out. Made a fucking mess as they were leaving too."

"How did they kill Senior?"

"Senior's property gutted him with his own knife. He was naked so she probably got him while he was on her. She let him bleed out and die. They took out Parrish at the door and shot and killed Fatz in the street, looked like they ran him over with a vehicle after. He was a fucking mess. I don't know where they got the vehicle so quick, or the weapons. Junior wants to talk to you about that."

"Me, why me?"

"You made a point of claiming that skank, even though you didn't have property rights. Junior just wants to ask you about it," Jazz said icily.

"I haven't been at base for the last couple days, I don't know what he wants from me," I said, but I followed Jazz out of my area and into the main building. You didn't argue when the new president summoned you.

Jazz led me straight to Junior's private area. It was only a bunch of tarps strung up between shelving from the grocery store, but it was bigger than the brothers' areas and he had a sofa in the corner and an actual mattress on the floor. He also had a coffee table set up to the side and was using it as a make-shift seat at the moment. Eagle was sitting on the sofa and he had another brother, one of his father's enforcers, Pink, standing up in the corner with his arms crossed Jazz tell ya?" Junior asked as I walked in, straight-forward as usual. He looked up at me, a smirk on his face. He didn't look like he was mourning his father's loss at all.

"That the girl Melinda escaped, yeah, he told me," I nodded.

"Yeah, that bitch got away. They broke the lock to the back room and she distracted Parrish from the front door. You got any idea how she would be able to do that?"

"None, Junior, I never really talked to her, if you know what I mean." It was a lie. I never had sex with Melinda and I actually liked her company, which was why I had begun to use my food credit to "buy" her for the night. I thought it would help me blend in better and give her a reprieve from the other men.

"See, I don't really know what ya mean, 'cause rumor was you never fucked her." Junior leaned forward, his blue eyes glinted white in the lantern light. Some of the women said he was attractive, but I didn't see it. He was fit and he liked to show it off by wearing tight black tees, but he was too hard looking, his tattoos too prison-like, his hair too greasy. He was the epitome of what I hated about this club.

"Bullshit," I spat. The lie tasted vile in my mouth, but it was necessary. I had learned quickly how to lie convincingly with this group. Junior was different though, at times he saw right through my deception. "Who's ever talking shit to you, Junior, they don't know what they're talking about."

"Jigger's old lady overheard that slut saying you let her sleep, didn't touch her. Plus, there ain't any sounds coming out of your berth when you get her back there. Sounds like y'all were up to something other than fucking, and with her escaping that's pretty suspicious, *Rebel*." He accentuated my name.

The name he gave me. Coined as an insult, rather than a compliment. In his eyes I was never one of the group. I was always rebelling against the system, the club. The club that he loved. I talked of college and a life with a real job. That was strange for Junior who only saw himself as the future president of the Southern Clan. To him I was different, a rebel, and the name stuck. When you rebel against the rebels - what does that make you?

"It was one fucking time. She had some kind of cold and I didn't want to get that shit. Who the fuck is up against my berth listening? That's fucked up, Junior. I never helped those girls escape, I had no clue, I wasn't even here. I was with Bear." Junior looked at me and then he looked at Jazz who nodded. All the cursing and lies tasted wrong in my mouth, but it was an act I had to maintain. I didn't like to use foul language, just as much as I didn't like to lie. I had tried to transition from my MC lifestyle when I was away at college. It was pathetic that I slipped back into it so easily.

"Fine, you were gone, out on watch," he scoffed and rolled his eyes like a child. Junior hadn't been on watch, once.

"Protecting this place, Junior, which is what I do every fucking day, more than the rest of this drug using-" It was too much, I stopped in mid-statement. I let my mouth get away from me all the time and it was dangerous with Junior.

"You always did have your fucking nose up in the air, Rebel. Better than the rest of us, college boy," he sneered. "No drugs for Rebel, no fucking either. Might as well be a fucking priest. I don't trust you, never did. You shouldn't have ever gotten those colors. I told Senior that, but he didn't listen. It was only because of your daddy that you got in. Your daddy should have taught you some fucking respect." He stood up and I knew I was screwed from the look on his face. He walked over to me and before I could react, he punched me in the gut.

The hit was hard and it made me bend over in reflex, gasping for air. I stood up quickly and faced him. I couldn't allow myself to show weakness to him. He never could take me down in a fight and he knew it. There was a reason he had his enforcer in the corner.

"You're tough, I'll give you that. I don't know if you had anything to do with those girls taking out Senior. I don't think I'll ever know, so I don't trust you, but you have your uses. Move your berth. You're going to take over Red's job guarding the fucking children. I'm wiping all your creds. No more women for you, Rebel. Hang out with the little kids and learn some respect. Maybe one day you can earn those fucking colors you wear. No more patrols either, you're on lockdown. Fuck up again and I'm stripping you. You'll be a fucking civilian."

With one move Junior had effectively neutered me. I was now in with the children. I wouldn't be able to leave the base, unless special permission was given and I would barely be able to leave the kids' area. Red was the oldest member of the club and he had been given the job because he couldn't do much more. It was a shit job. A job that would usually fall to the women, but no one in the club trusted the women enough to let them carry. And the children needed to be protected.

I walked out of Junior's area without saying a word. He knew what he was doing. If he suspected me of any kind of malicious behavior then he had me where he could keep me in my place. The kids' area was always under guard with a constant rotation of brothers. It would be the first place the civilians went if they were to break free, so they had to have it watched. There was always a guard inside and one that rotated at the back door. The one inside acted as the nanny and watched the women that were allowed to come in and tend to the kids.

It was a shit position. I was now the glorified babysitter.

FIVE

AMPHIBIOUS ASS-KICKER

BABY

Trivox was a production facility about five miles from our compound that had produced vehicles for the U.S. military. They specialized in armored land and marine vehicles along with a few weapon systems. It wasn't a huge facility, but we were hoping that they would be stocked with a good base of weaponry.

Our group hadn't even considered scavenging in the manufacturing plants that ran along Lake Pontchartrain since most of them were full of tools and materials that we wouldn't be able to use. They held nothing sustainable like food or water, but we had forgotten about Trivox. Weapons we could use.

The plant had been closed on the Saturday that Z hit, so on our initial scouting we only noticed a few Zs wandering around in the yard, still in their security uniforms. The company must have recently shipped out a lot of their stock since there were only a few of their armored SCTVs in the lot. An SCTV or Survivable Combat Tactical Vehicle, were armored vehicles that were slowly replacing the Humvees. They were cheaper and took a hit better.

We were going in as a team. The mission was to go in fast, take out any of the dead and secure weapons and vehicles as quickly as possible. Our forward team consisted of Romeo, whose nickname was worse than mine, Vance Ito, who we called Ito, Jimmy and Blake. We cut into the chain-link fence that surrounded the place and I whistled to attract the attention of the two Zs that were roaming the yard.

They approached us like good little dead things and we dispatched them easily. I didn't even have to take out my Bowie because Jimmy and Ito were on it, fast and efficient.

We split up to case the area, looking for an easily accessible entry point. We wanted to enter the plant and not have to search around for the storage area. More chances to have a dead worker surprise us if we wandered around the offices looking for a door into the warehouse. Getting in was probably going to be the hardest process. It was a government contractor so they were locked down tight, not many windows and the doors were reinforced. Most of their security relied on electricity though, so once we found an entrance that looked suitable it only took a crowbar and a bit of muscle to pry open the door.

Our banging and scratching to get in drew the attention of the Saturday workers; they were ready for us when the door swung open. A flood of hungry and bedraggled zombies poured out the small entry way. They were actually in better condition than the ones left out in the elements. They were oddly dry, with crusty looking skin, instead of the oozing, wet look we were used to.

Most of them looked like the typical business types in polos and khakis for the Saturday grind, but a few seemed to be workers, possibly the cleaning staff, because they wore coveralls. They reached for us with their mouths opened wide. Their dry, brittle skin looked like it could crack and break away if you touched it wrong. Appearances could be deceiving though, I knew better, they were tougher than they looked. Their grips were like steel. They would pull you to them with a tenacity fueled by some unknown element that kept them alive.

I holstered my piece and pulled out my Bowie knife. I grabbed for the closest and pulled it to me, embedding my knife in its skull. The skin looked dry, but it had a weird consistency, almost like leather. I didn't know what had caused them to decompose like this, but it was bizarre. A chunk of hair came off in my hand and I shook it off as the body fell to my feet. I tried to kick it away, but it was a solid male and I only moved it slightly. I didn't have time to mess around, there were more coming, so I stepped over the body and grabbed for another.

This one got a good grip on my shoulder and I had to push my arm up toward its face to keep the teeth away from my exposed skin. I had wrapped my arms in the hillbilly armor we had perfected at the compound, a mix of leather and repurposed rubber tires to keep teeth from finding exposed flesh. When I didn't have to worry about bites it made it easier to take them out. You couldn't cover everything, though. I stabbed upward and took it out with a quick jab to the temple.

I took down two more and was finally able to take a breath. The herd was culled as Ito dropped the last one at his feet. Blake clicked on a torch and signaled for us to follow him into the dark building.

We encountered two more Zs on the way to the plant floor, but those weren't enough of a challenge to even get my heart rate up. When we found the door that led to the big production room floor, where hopefully the vehicles were stored, we clicked off our lights and entered as silently as possible. There was enough natural light coming in from windows high above us to see without the use of the flashlights.

The room was large, big enough and tall enough to fit a few commercial airliners. Motors and engine parts lined the far wall and a good amount of half-constructed vehicles sat to the right of us. The back wall opened to a large bay door that could open and close to about four feet above the ground. The bay door was large and most of it was over the water of a pool and docking area. The pool fed into the lake so the LCACs that were docked inside could be driven out into the lake for testing.

We had thought about taking an LCAC, but they were too much. The LCACs were big. They required a crew and could carry ten land vehicles and a whole regiment. It would be like firing up a destroyer and taking it into Lakeview. We needed something smaller that could be manned by one or two of our people.

"Jimmy and Ito, check out the water, see if there's anything we can use," Blake said and the two peeled off and headed toward the docks.

"I want the rest of us in an SCTV, it looks like they have enough," he gestured to the group of tan vehicles to the left of us.

"Get the garage doors up, Ba–*Hannah*." I glared at him for almost calling me Baby, then I followed his orders and went to the doors. They were electrical but there was always a way around.

It took a bit of poking, but I found the manual release and disengaged the rail, allowing me to pull on the rope and bring the door up. It was big and I was huffing from the weight, by the time it was all the way up, but I got that bitch open and managed to engage the latch to keep it from crashing down.

I heard the crank of a few engines and fell back to find my own armored vehicle. I had secretly hoped they had a tank or two. I always wanted to drive a tank–but it was nothing but these armored vehicles. They didn't even have mounted .50 calibers, which was rather disappointing.

My com crackled with static, Ito and Jimmy had found something. Jimmy's voice came over the small speaker, "We got a small craft, looks like maybe a prototype or something they were engineering for a private customer. It's not military. Can only hold five vehicles at max and has the controls of a regular craft. We can handle this one. It's berth five. We can load a few of the SCTVs onto it."

"Good job, Jimmy. Romeo and I will meet you down there with two of these vehicles." The com clicked off as I walked to Blake. He was paging through a binder.

"Looks like they only have vehicles. The weaponry must be attached at another plant, this is it. Number eight-seven over there should be gassed up. Take that one out into the yard," he said to me. "Romeo, take number nine-two down to the docks. I'll follow in eight-three. We can come back and grab those two," He pointed at the ones closest to us, "And follow Baby out." I let him slide this time with the name and walked to my assigned vehicle without a glare. I was getting better.

The keys were in the ignition, the benefits of being in a locked plant, and the machine started right up. It wasn't exactly like driving a truck, but it wasn't rocket science either. I revved the engine and rolled out. Looks like the S-Island crew were now militarized.

SIX

HOUSEKEEPING

REBEL

The babysitter was in the house.

There were only about eighteen children. They ranged in age from seven to fifteen. I hadn't had much contact with the kids, didn't have any reason to. It wasn't like I had any kids myself, or knew any of them personally. They mostly belonged to civilians, only three of them were legacy children and they were mainly tended by the old ladies and kept in another location.

They greeted me suspiciously when I moved my box of possessions into the building. Red had told them he was leaving, which if I was one of those kids, I would think it was a positive. Red wasn't exactly the cuddly and kid-friendly type.

The oldest boy, a scrawny fifteen-year-old, showed me to Red's old berth and I tried not to think about how oily he was when I looked at the cot.

"What did Red do all day?" I asked the boy.

"Nothing. He sat around complaining and he distributed the food when they sent it back for us," he said quietly.

This was going to be boring.

I spent the rest of the evening checking out the place. The building was secure. It had been a gym, but all the machines had been moved into the back parking lot. The front was all glass and overlooked the front lot where the civilian men lived and worked. The entire parking area was surrounded by a chain-link fence.

There was only one exit in the back, a rear door that was guarded by one of the brothers day and night. Or it was supposed to be. Mostly it was locked from the outside and there was no way to look out and check if someone was standing there.

Realistically if I were to make a break for it, it would be through the back door. The back parking lot led right into a residential area and I could slip away quickly without being noticed. But I would have to break the lock and hope there wasn't a guard on the back door.

For now I would have to feel out my new role and hope that an opportunity opened up and I could slip away.

The place was a sty, old food and trays were piled up in the back. Red had probably been waiting for one of the women to clean it up for him. Old candles had been allowed to burn down to nothing and pool wax over counters and tables. I even found a stash of food that Red was hiding from the rest of the group. It was kid stuff, like gummy bears and stale Pop Tarts, obviously intended for the children. Red must have forgotten about it since I found it under a pile of paper in the corner, discarded like trash.

You would have thought it was Christmas when I handed it out to the kids. It had no nutritional value, but they were happy. At first they were suspicious, but as the first taste of sugar melted on their tongues, they became giddy. Kids were easy to please.

After the sugar party, I continued to clean up the place, throwing everything in a cardboard box I found by the back door. There were plastic cups everywhere and toys in every corner of the place. I was mostly concerned about the old food and the state of the bathrooms. It wasn't healthy. I guess I could keep busy by getting it in order. There was no way I could think in this mess.

Babysitter and now housekeeper. My life kept improving.

SEVEN

COMPLICATED SUCKS

BABY

We rolled up on the compound like an invading army. Ito and Jimmy's trip was longer and over water, so it was just us rolling in. We still got treated with a crowd running out to greet us and applause as we entered the compound.

We were rendezvousing with the troopers and the dregs of the National Guard tomorrow and we would roll into Lakeview that night. So, all we had to do was load up and get some rest.

Blake and Zach wanted to leave some fighters back at the compound, in case something happened while we were gone, but most of us were heading to Lakeview.

"I'm assuming we're leaving Peters on the island," I said to Zach as we walked into the main building of our compound. Cole Peters was another MJ grunt, but he was the only one that had kids and a wife at the compound. He was a good fighter, but his wife Grace liked him to stay close to home. I didn't blame her. If I was her, I would want my husband staying home and protecting me and the kids too.

"Right. Peters, Hank Voiter, Justin Crisps, Ray, Orlando and Liam are all staying back. They're all a good shot, but if something happens, it'll be bad. I don't want to think about that possibility. Most of the women are staying back. I only have Alexis, Melinda, you and Lani in the mix to go to Lakeview. Barbara Voiter and Madison have been training on and off with Kirk, which will leave the compound with eight guns, nine if you count Bubba, guarding nine children and two non-combat adults. We have to make this Lakeview mission quick, I don't feel comfortable with those odds."

"You're leaving Clara here?" I had done the math. The two non-combat adults were Clara and Patricia. The useless females in our group. Clara was kept locked in the infirmary because she had tried to kill Alexis. Didn't want a repeat of that situation. And Patricia was a self-declared pacifist, which meant she didn't even help fish. Useless.

"Yeah, she stays locked up. We're going to move her after we take Lakeview," Blake said, his face hard and unreadable.

I didn't like the drama that revolved around Blake, Zach and Alexis. I got that they were happy, that they had found their thing. But to me it was a little too much. I despised drama of any kind.

Relationships meant drama. Their trio had it in spades since more people in the mix meant more issues. I didn't quite get their dynamic. I didn't think Blake and Zach were together, I never got that vibe from them. It was all about Lex. More power to her. I might not understand having a relationship with two men at once, but it was jealousy inducing. Having two hot guys fawn all over you, a girl could only wish. I couldn't handle it in real life, but it made for a nice fantasy. I can't even handle one. Even one was too much drama for me.

Then you add Clara to the mix and I think that's where I want to call and all-stop.

Clara, the one locked in the infirmary, had tried to kill Lex. Clara, Blake's ex-wife. Crazy ex-wife. The kind of ex-wife you would describe as manipulative, obsessive– homicidal. Nuttier than my Aunt Cookie, who's a paranoid schizophrenic, so that's saying a lot.

Clara had done everything in her power to get Blake back, which is where all the drama had come in. She had even faked a pregnancy, talked her way into making him rescue her in Texas and leaving Alexis and Zach behind. Then, when he brought her back here, with a few other survivors in tow, she had the audacity to try and kill Alexis because she didn't like the competition.

She thought if Lex was out of the picture she would be Blake's number one again. Love makes people do stupid shit. It didn't win over Blake, it had the opposite effect, Blake was devastated and hadn't been the same since.

The whole situation is FUBAR and poor Blake was caught in the middle. Yeah, it was partly his fault, and he got Lex back and they're all loved up in their happy trio, but now he has to figure out what to do with Clara. She might be batshit, but she's also his ex and I'm sure he loved her at some point. He's got his ex locked in an infirmary right now. You can tell it's bugging the crap out of him.

"And then what do you plan on doing with her?" I asked curious. Personally, I thought she should be taken out and shot, it would solve a lot of problems, but I was in the minority.

"Poche and Ryan want to set up a court system once we get things settled in Lakeview. We'll have prisoners from the siege. Hopefully most of them will surrender without a fight. Each one will be tried, Poche and Ryan plan to sit on the court along with a representative from our group, maybe one grunt and one civilian."

"Wow, that's like civilized and shit," I coughed, thinking it was a waste of time. These were lowlifes that were holding women prisoner and raping them on demand. There was no question to their guilt or innocence, all of them should be taken out. "So, what, y'all vote guilty or innocent? What happens if you vote guilty?"

"Firing squad," Blake said simply.

"And innocent?" He shrugged.

"What if it's a tie, if you have four on the panel, that could lead to some debate?" I asked.

"I think it should be five at the least, to avoid that," he sighed. I could tell he wasn't too won over by this idea either.

"If you have two military and one police representative, you should probably have two civilian representatives to even it out. One male and one female. That seems logical."

"Logical is good, right?" He laughed.

"Logic is telling me to firebomb those shitholes and call it a wash."

"They have about fifteen kids in there, not to mention the innocent women and men that they have doing their labor for them. It's always a lot more complicated than we want it to be," he said.

I looked at Blake. He had changed a lot since Lex had been kidnapped. It wasn't just his new high and tight. He was always the more laid back of my bosses, quick to smile and dish out a joke or break out a bottle of liquor. But now the smiles were few and far between. I only saw him smile when Lex was near. When they were apart, the worry was evident in everything he did. I knew he loved her, but if this was what love did to you, stressed you out and had you all worried when they weren't near, count me out.

I worried about my fellow survivors, but I liked putting me as number one on the list. It was hard enough keeping myself alive. It would blow being constantly worried about someone else.

"Complicated sucks," I mumbled.

"We'll figure it out," Blake said assuredly, finally a hint of a smile playing on his lips as he looked at me.

"We get to start again. We've got to do it right. Let's round up everyone and get packed up. Only a few more hours until we fall out," he said in his stern, boss voice.

"I hope it's worth it," I whispered as he walked away from me down the hall. It was hard finding meaning in this new life. It was harder to think that one day our struggles might end and we might go back to worrying about trivial things.

I was pretty sure I wouldn't live to see that day. Lifespans were considerably limited in this new world. I was destined to catch up to Martinez sooner rather than later. Lucas Martinez was the last MJ grunt we lost to the Z. He bit it when we were trying to rescue Lex from Lakeview. He had only died a few weeks ago, it still hurt to think about it. I knew that sooner, rather than later, that would be me.

Maybe in a few decades the dead will rot away and the remaining humanity can pick up the pieces. Start over again. It would be nothing like the world we left behind, though. I could pretty much guarantee that. That world was long gone.

EIGHT

PRETTY WORDS WITH NO MEANING

REBEL

I fell into a routine. The children didn't need much. They were well-behaved, forced into obedience because of their dreary existence. There were plenty of toys. They had the pick of everything that was scavenged from the drug store on the corner. Most of the time they were content to play quietly, only getting excited when one of the women or civilian men were brought in. They would jump to their feet when the door creaked open. Each one hoping it was their mother or father. Their faces would pinch up in eager anticipation, not wanting to look happy, but not able to hide their hope.

When they would spot their parent, the lucky child would break into tears or a shout and rush to the adult. The others would wipe at their faces and sit back down, going back to their game or activity. It was heart-breaking.

Most of my time was spent idle. I distracted myself by using the punching bag that was bolted into the floor and ceiling. They hadn't been able to remove it, so it worked in my favor. I also spent a lot of time playing cards. The older kids, two boys and one girl, got over their initial shyness and started hovering around me, so I taught them a few games and they quickly kicked my butt.

When we got tired of cards, I started teaching them a few self-defense tactics using the bag and the open floor. They were eager and willing to fight, even the girl. They knew their survival meant being able to defend themselves. We had to keep it a secret, though, I would have gotten us all in trouble if someone found out about our lessons.

The girl was named Felicity. She was a pretty little thing, but underweight, which I had to admit was a good thing. She was fourteen and on the verge of womanhood. Being underweight kept her curves hidden from the brothers. It wasn't good to be a woman in this place.

The boys were Nick and Pete, twelve and fifteen respectively, both small and immature in their behavior but grave at the same time. They were good company, if a bit on the quiet side. We were playing a game of poker when the back door opened and one of the civilian men came in with the day's rations. I stood and motioned for the teens to continue without me.

Eagle escorted the man inside and walked up to me, his eyes glancing behind my back and lingering on the teens. I stepped in front of him, not liking the way his lips curved into a smirk when he made eye contact with me. He was here to check in on me.

"How ya doing, man?" he asked with insincerity.

"Bored," I said.

"Yeah, shit detail, didn't know what else to do with you. You gotta shoot straight or this is where you'll stay," he said and grinned. He liked that I was here. He was a cruel one. I didn't know who was worse, him or Junior.

"I don't know what else I could have done, Eagle. I didn't help those chicks get out and I never did anything but protect this place, same thing I'm doing now." I shook my head.

"Don't play stupid with me, Rebel. You always think you're so smart, trying to get one over on all of us. Junior and me, though– we got your number. We know your heart ain't with the Clan. We can see it every time you talk, every move you make. Until we know you put the Clan first, above all else, you're not gonna be trusted. You're lucky he didn't strip ya, I would've."

"I do put the Clan first," I lied.

"See, I don't believe you," he shrugged. "It's like when I used to tell bitches I loved them just to bag them, pretty words, nothing behind it."

"Well, I don't know what you want from me, Eagle. Just tell me what Junior wants and I'll handle it. I'm here, aren't I? How else can I prove it?"

"Like you handled that beating? Or how you handled that back-up before the biters took over?" He brought up something from our teen years, when I was asked to run back-up for a drug deal with another club. I had refused. I had gotten my college acceptance papers and I didn't want to risk my future. They had discussed stripping me then, but my father had intervened with the argument that the club did need college graduates. He told them I was going to be a lawyer so I could handle their legal issues. They beat me anyway. Bad. I was lucky I finished high school. I spent the remainder of my senior year in the hospital.

I had nothing to say to Eagle and he nodded in understanding. Refusing your brothers was akin to being a traitor. There was no grey with this group, only black and white.

"Like I was saying, you don't put the Clan first, you look out for one thing, and that's your pretty little ass," he laughed and slapped me hard on the back, putting a bit more force into it than he needed to.

"Speaking of pretty little asses, that one looks like she should be in the rotation," he said and pointed to Felicity. My stomach sank.

"She's too young. Senior said none under seventeen," I stated firmly. "She's only twelve," I lied again.

"She's don't look twelve," he leered. "Maybe I'll make Junior change the rule."

"They got plenty of experienced women in the back, Eagle. Why you want one that'll lay there and cry?" I tried to sound reasonable.

"Yeah, you're right." He looked over my shoulder again and I cringed.

"Really, let me know if there is anything I can do. I'm not as selfish as you guys think," I said changing the subject.

"Sure." He cocked his head and looked at me again, probably trying to get a read on whether I was serious. Satisfied, he grunted and turned and left, motioning for the civilian to follow him out.

As soon as the door closed, I went to find a pair of scissors.

NINE

FUCK YEAH

BABY

We had an early morning reveille at four a.m. No bugle. We were treated to Zach screaming at the top of his lungs, "Fall out, assholes!"

I was used to early morning drills, so I was down and dressed in minutes. I stood by Zach's side and urged everyone on, donning my drill sergeant persona. It was growing on me.

"Y'all suck," Alexis said as she walked past us, a large pack on her back and an M4 in front of her.

"You look fucking sexy with that rifle," Zach said and grabbed her, planting a kiss on her roughly.

"Get a room," I grumbled and avoided the two of them as they got into the kiss. I tried not to stare, but a little part of me wished I was in Lex's place, a guy fawning all over me and wanting me desperately.

The part of me that I liked to mock and throw stuff at.

"Meet ya in the truck," Zach ended the kiss and swatted her on the ass.

She turned and rushed down the hallway and out into the yard with a haughty smirk thrown my way. She knew PDA bothered me.

"You're like a horny teenager. I've lost all respect for you, just so you know," I said as we walked into the chilly morning.

"Jealousy doesn't suit you, Baby."

"Fuck you, boss," I flipped him off.

The three SCTVs were idling in the yard, waiting for their drivers. Ito, Jimmy, and Isaiah were going by water, with one of the armored vehicles loaded. We were leaving one here for the compound. I was going in the rig with Romeo and Lani. The second rig held Lex, Zach, and Blake. The third rig was driven by Kirk and held Duke and Bret Klein.

The goal was to meet up with the troopers and the National Guard in a house off St. Bernard Avenue and Filmore that the group had cleared and were using as a secondary base. Another team from the troopers would break off and hook up with the water craft at a park off Lakeshore Drive, close to Lakeview.

Ito would come in from the rear and we would come in from the main road with a direct assault. Hopefully, it would lead to a bunch of bikers peeing their pants and giving up like the pussies they were. Hopefully.

As we crossed the causeway that separated our compound from the main drag, I settled into the uncomfortable seat and closed my eyes to catch a few minutes of much needed rest.

Romeo didn't talk and Lani was uncharacteristically quiet, so I slipped into a half doze. Lani usually talked my ear off, a constant barrage of questions about everything and anything. How to do this, and what was it like to do this or that? Poor thing hadn't lived much before Z hit. She was a sheltered teenager and never got to explore the world before Z, much less live in it. Her quiet nervousness made me twitchy.

I cracked my eye when a large pothole jolted the vehicle and threw me into the door.

"Fuck! Watch it, Romeo," I growled.

"It was unavoidable," he responded.

"It wasn't his fault," Lani defended him. "The thing was huge. Come summer the streets are going to be a mess."

New Orleans was a swamp. Our streets and houses were built on unstable ground. During the summer the cement heated up and expanded. Fissures in the road often appeared and huge potholes formed overnight. Before Z, the city didn't fix many of the potholes that formed, unless they became a hazard, leading a lot of New Orleans residents to bitch and get little signs to put in their yard that said, "Fix our streets." Now there was no one to fill them in, even if there was an inclination. We'd be reduced to expanses of crumbling cement in only a few short years.

"I remember there was this big pothole, probably more of a sinkhole than a pothole. It formed right outside of our school, and it was so funny. Someone put a flamingo in there and then during Christmas they decorated the flamingo. What part of the city did you live in before Z, Ro–Romeo?" She faltered on his name, which had alarm bells going off in my head.

I was trying to shut them out and go back to sleep, but something about the way Lani was carrying on had me feigning sleep. I felt kind of protective of her. She was a sweet girl and worked her ass off, something I respected. She was also really young and naive. I didn't want her to get grumpy and jaded like me.

Men tended to bring out the jadedness in most women. Whether it's Daddy, or that first awful love, most of the time it's a guy that fucks us up royally. Romeo was every girl's fantasy. He had even starred in a few of mine, before I got to know him. Hopefully Lani would realize he was bad news and find someone more in her sphere. She didn't need to go there.

"Mid-City," he answered tersely.

"We used to live in the city, but my dad moved us to Metairie after the crime got out of hand. My mom was robbed in our driveway." She looked over at Romeo with that star struck look you only see in young girls and old people with dementia.

This wasn't good. Not good at all.

Romeo had been something else before Z. A perfect male specimen. When I got the job at MJ Security, he was the first one I heard about. He and Lucas Martinez had been with Blake and Zach from the start. They were all Marines and part of the same regiment. Romeo was an MJ Security icon when I got there. Known as an adrenaline junkie, he took the hardest, most dangerous jobs Zach and Blake had for him. Before I met him, I had already heard a hundred stories. The other grunts told tales of his exploits like he was a superhero.

It didn't help that he was unbelievably gorgeous. One of the prettiest men I've ever laid eyes on. By the time I met him in person, I was ready to kick off my panties and take him for a test drive. Not part of my usual routine, so it had even me scratching my head. Luckily though, Romeo opened his mouth and ruined it for me.

He was such an egotistical bastard. It was almost refreshing. And it pushed him firmly in my no-touch zone. A girl couldn't carry-on with a guy prettier than her. I was also sure he felt the same way about me. Not the prettier part. The no-touch part. He half-heartedly flirted at first, but it was nothing like what I saw him try with other women. It was almost like an art form. The other guys would take notes.

Then Z hit. And something happened to Romeo. He was still gorgeous. He was still an adrenaline junkie. He was still the first one to run into the shit, but there was no more play in him. There was no more ego. Or flirting. He was this stoic, mysterious, gorgeous hero. With the brooding bit, he's even more of a turn-on than he was before.

We had been a fun group, before Z. You would have thought it would be awkward, but it wasn't, me being the only female in a group of Alpha men. We had been a great team. A group that worked, but most of all, everyone knew how to have a good time. Now all my guys had lost that fun, that spark. It had started when Z hit, but the final nail was when Martinez died.

All stop. Didn't want to think about that.

There was a point to my meandering thoughts and it all came back to the fact that Lani should stay far away from Romeo. For one, she was way too young, and two, she didn't need a broken man. And there was no question, Romeo was broken.

"How did you get your nickname?" Lani was desperately trying to make conversation, even though Romeo was down to only grunts.

"Long story," Romeo responded. She should be grateful she got two words out of him.

"Seems we have time," she said and motioned to the convoy in front of us which was creeping along at a snail's pace. Ahead of us, Lex was leaning out the window trying to stick a shuffling zombie with a spear.

If she fell out of the vehicle, I was going to kill her.

"It's not that long of a story," I yawned. "Romeo was quite a ladies' man. He could charm the panties off any female and probably a few men. All he had to do was flash that pretty smile. Problem with Romeo, he never could find his Juliet- he sure did try, though. Over and over again," I laughed. "And over again."

He shook his head but didn't deny it.

Lani turned around in her seat and gave me an ugly look, I shrugged. It was the truth.

"I didn't expect that," she laughed nervously, trying to cover up her obvious disappointment. "Is that true?" she asked Romeo.

"That about covers it." He cocked his head and made some adjustments as the brake lights of the lead vehicle flashed. The conversation didn't phase him. Since Z I hadn't seen him break a sweat about anything. "Lead, come back," he said into the radio.

"Just got a small herd ahead of us, nothing to worry about," Zach said through the radio.

I dug through my bag and pulled out a newly acquired Maxim 9 that I had talked Zach into letting me use. It was from his personal stash, the first line of guns made of its kind with the suppressor built into the barrel. It looked all sci-fi with a large square shaped muzzle, but it fired regular 9mm rounds and had a decent sized clip.   I was dying to use it and now was my chance.

I unlatched the access point in the roof and slid the door back. Bright sunlight filtered in, the sun now completely up. I stood in my seat, bracing myself with the built in handhelds made for this action. I had a 360 view of my surroundings. I only had to stay aware of Romeo's driving so I wouldn't fall forward. The vehicle was meant to have a large .50 caliber mounted to the roof where the operator could hang on to the gun. It wasn't meant to balance and shoot a handgun, but I was a girl that liked to live on the edge.

I saw Alexis push out the top of the vehicle in front of us. She turned around and screamed, "Fuck yeah!" And gave me a thumbs up sign.

Then the lead vehicle revved its engine and pushed forward through the large group of the dead. Some fell under the tires, others began to swarm around the vehicles.

I took aim and fired.

Headshot. Down it went.

Aim. Fire. Headshot. *Fuck yeah is right.*

Aim. Fire. Miss. *Shit.* Three more taps and it finally went down.

The suppressor on the gun muffled the shot so it sounded like a loud pop, instead of a deafening boom. It was still enough noise to attract the attention of more zombies, but Lex shot that all to hell when she chose her semi-automatic M4 and was taking them down in three round bursts.

"Stop playing around with the fucking nine," Romeo called to me from below.

I felt something hit my kneecap, Romeo jabbed me with the rifle to get my attention. I ducked down and grabbed the rifle from his hand and shrugged an apology. I engaged the safety on the Maxim and dropped it into the backseat and pulled up the M4. I could operate this weapon in my sleep. It was like shooting fish in a barrel after that and when only a few remained and the lead vehicle sped up, leaving a trail of dead Zs in our wake, I sat down and secured my weapon.

"Next time you're driving," Romeo declared as he caught my eye in the rearview mirror. I was smiling from ear to ear. I needed that.

"Don't worry, hotness, they'll be plenty of action for you later." I sat low in my seat, catching a glimpse of Lani's scowl in my peripheral. *She needed to get over that shit, fast.*

TEN

NO BETTER

REBEL

"Why do you want me to cut my hair?" Felicity whined as Nick and Pete stared on looking anxious.

"I'm going to play it straight with you." I kneeled in front of the young girl whose beautiful brunette hair was probably the only thing she had left to be proud of in this world. It was long and she brushed it every day, leaving it loose and down her back. It wasn't quite as shiny as it could be, and the ends were frayed, but it was still beautiful. *It had to go.*

"You don't want boys to look at you and admire your looks in this place, Felicity. It's not a good thing. Not like it used to be. Before the biters you could be pretty, you could be a little girl, pretending to be a woman and it was okay. People still respected that you were young and waited for you to grow up. You only had to worry about a few perverts, men you saw on the news. Now, in here, there are no rules, no jails for men to fear and the men that run this camp are like those men on the news. In this place, pretty means a possession, it means something to be possessed. Pretty means you belong to a man. Pretty means a man can do things to you that you don't want him to do. If you say no, it won't mean anything to these men. They don't care about you or your feelings. They only care about how you look and how you make them feel. I don't want you to cut your hair to punish you. I think cutting your hair will give you more time. More time to be young. And maybe when you're old enough things will be different. You'll be able to have your hair long and not worry about it attracting the wrong attention. Do you understand?"

"I think so. Is that why they keep my mom away from me? Do they keep her like property?"

I didn't know which one was her mother, and I hadn't seen anyone come in and greet her like a parent.

"Yes, and they don't treat their property well, you know this, right? Look how they treat you guys. But once you become an adult in their eyes, all bets are off. They can do anything they want," I said quietly. A single tear leaked from her eye and trailed down her face. She wiped at it absently and chewed her bottom lip, looking from Nick to Pete. They both encouraged her with a nod.

"I don't even want to think about that," she said under her breath.

"We have to, that man that was in here earlier, Eagle. He'll come back and if he sees a pretty girl, he'll want to move you out of the kids' area and in with the women. You have to cover yourself up. Wear oversized shirts, chop your hair off." She pulled the scissors out of my hand and looked to the boys.

"You can't look like a woman, Felicity. No matter what. There can be nothing sexual about you, no curves, no pretty hair, no cute behavior. I can't stress that enough." I felt like the bad guy who drew back the curtain and ruined Christmas.

"I'll help," Pete said and led her away.

"If they're like this, if they're so bad, treat women like this, why are you with them? Why do you wear their patches all over you?" Nick asked angrily. I was a little shocked by the vehemence in his voice. It was the first time he had shown any kind of backbone.

"I'm as much a prisoner as everyone else here," I said in return.

"Bullshit," he stood up abruptly. "You came in with them. Before you were assigned here you were out there, doing what they do. You screwed up, that's why they put you here. I heard Red talking about it. Don't pretend you're better than them. You wear their patches, you're one of them." He stomped away, following Pete and Felicity to the bathroom.

I deserved that. I deserved every bit of it. I was a coward. The only way I stood up to these men was with a bit of back talk. Stupid words that didn't mean anything. I might as well be a part of it. I stood back and let them do whatever they wanted to do, calling myself moral because in my head I opposed their actions. When really I was a selfish coward. I was only thinking about myself. I had been focused on my escape. Never thinking of the other people caught up in this mess.

I was always focused on my own situation, never once thinking about how I could end this mess. The women here were slaves, treated worse than dogs. The civilian men were kept around so they could work for the Clan. Slaves. The children were held to keep everyone in check.

I was no better than them. Just because I was a rebel in my head, morally opposing their actions, didn't make me any less responsible for this mess. *But what could I do?*

It was me versus forty armed men. They would kill me if I tried to do anything to save these people.

Maybe it was what I deserved. Death would probably be the only escape I got. If I took out a few along the way, would that redeem me?

Nick's anger haunted me even as I slept that night.

ELEVEN

THE ASSHOLE IN CHARGE

BABY

In under two hours we crossed from the neighborhood of Gentilly into Lake Vista without any more issues. We passed a good number of the dead, but nothing like the herd in New Orleans East.

We drove the all-terrain vehicles over lawns, neutral grounds and even through over-grown fields to avoid stalled cars and random road blocks.

The vehicles in the road were beginning to rust, and they were covered in so much dirt and debris they looked ancient. Houses were hidden by overgrown weeds and tall grass, the fast-growing trees and shrubs all but obscuring most houses. There were no more lawns and neat sidewalks. New Orleans resembled the apocalyptic landscape it was. I thought I had seen the worst after Katrina. I wasn't from New Orleans, I grew up mostly around the Pensacola area in Florida. At the time of Katrina I was staying with a foster family that considered themselves religious and they had made the trek to New Orleans to help rebuild with their church group. They had brought me with them, citing it as a learning experience.

The three months we stayed here after the storm changed my life forever.

It was why I moved here after I left the Army, why I chose to return to this tragic city that had finally begun to return to normal. The city had finally begun stretching out, finding its place, when the world collapsed under the onslaught of the dead.

After the floods from Hurricane Katrina, the houses had been a mess, like someone had come in and shook everything up and drenched them in mud. But there was life. There were people within the houses. There were sounds of power tools and the hum of military vehicles. Hammers and the tinny sound of music.

I remember sitting on a discarded and taped up refrigerator eating red beans and rice out of a Styrofoam to-go plate delivered by the Red Cross. I remember sitting there, looking at the destruction around me, while the sound of a brass band filtered down the street. *And I never felt more at ease.* Because in the midst of that destruction, people came together. People stopped and chatted with each other. They cried in the street and held on to complete strangers. They looked at their devastated city and had hope. Hope for the future. It was inspiring.

This was the exact opposite. There was no hope here. There was no future. The dead had turned on the living and the living were tearing each other to shreds.

After the storm, I had heard the stories. A local I had befriended had whispered to me about how he had heard the gangs were going through the neighborhoods that weren't flooded and pulling people from their houses and beating them, then robbing them. How the National Guard was shooting and asking questions later. There had still been that underlying danger.

But, I didn't see that. I saw the good and it stuck with me. It was why

I joined the Army. It was why I returned to New Orleans after all those years and it's why when I looked around at this abandoned city, crumbling under neglect, it hurt me physically. It was hard seeing the city I loved slowly die. It was hard not having any hope for a future.

"Head's up, we've gotta come in quiet. First street over the bayou, hang a right," Blake's voice crackled over the radio.

We crossed Bayou St. John and took an immediate right, following the lead vehicle down a side street and then hanging another right into a cul de sac.

The streets were empty, no cars even in the driveways, as if someone had deliberately cleared the area. The lead vehicle pulled to the end of the street and parked in the turn. Romeo pulled up behind the first vehicle and I glanced at the house that stood watch at the end of the block. It really wasn't a house, more of a mansion. It looked to be almost four stories and in better condition than the houses around it.

The grass and weeds were all dead around the house, leaving only an expanse of dirt, with the sidewalk showing, a first. It was cracked and splintered like most New Orleans sidewalks, but it was at least able to be seen.

I saw motion in the windows and the front door opened, revealing Poche, the man that had taken up the role of leader to the remaining National Guardsmen in the city.

Poche was older than the rest of us, and if you could trust the chevrons on the uniform he wore, he was a First Sergeant. That meant he was probably in his early forties and had served his twenty. He took pride in his rank. His uniform was worn, but clean, and he held himself like the noncommissioned officer he was. His hair was still tight, his boots still shined. He probably was forced to keep himself military rigid if he wanted to retain control of his men. Any sign of weakness and they would fall apart. In a situation like this, he would have to give them some kind of normalcy and a rigid military atmosphere would do that.

Blake and Zach were out of their vehicle and striding across the lawn, while the rest of us held back and waited for our orders.

"I guess this is it, after we get them in place, we're going into Lakeview," Lani said quietly. She had exited the vehicle and was stretching her back, the SCTV wasn't the most comfortable ride.

"Yup, you know you don't have to do this, right?" I looked at her. Lani was the only person in our compound, besides the kids, that I could meet eye to eye.

"I'm doing this, Hannah," she said with more resolve than could be seen on her face.

"We're letting the soldiers go in first, though, I don't want you playing the hero. You've only been training for a couple weeks. We've been training for years. All of the MJ grunts have done a couple tours. We'll need you to help secure the women and children, Lani. If you go in and put yourself at risk, you'll endanger not only yourself, but one of us who will have to save you."

"I won't do anything stupid. I know my place." She frowned and looked at Romeo who had popped the hood and was looking at the engine.

"Don't say it like that. You don't want to be like us, Lani. We've been broken a million times over. Every time you kill someone it breaks off bits of your soul and replaces it with something dark and cold. You don't want that, you don't want any part of that. We make it look big and heroic, but really it's lonely and heavy." My words surprised me. I was being a total drama queen. Lex was rubbing off on me.

"I want to help, I want to make things right."

"You'll help. You know the women, they'll see you and trust us. You'll get them to safety. You'll help get the children out, they are the priority. We'll worry about the nasty things; you worry about saving lives."

"Well, when you say it like that," she laughed lightly.

A young soldier caught my eye, his uniform was messy and he only wore the one chevron of a Private 2nd Class. He had barely made it out of boot camp, if that was his true rank and not a scavenged uniform. He walked up to Blake and saluted him, which was ridiculous.

Blake shook his hand to stop the private and then motioned in my direction. The soldier came running over to me with an eager look on his face. I looked at Blake who was trying to hold back a laugh, and I could only imagine what this was going to be about.

"Hey, uh, I'm Morel," he greeted me and stuck his hand out. I took it gingerly. "The Sergeant told me that you would be my team leader, that we would be going in with you."

"Great, Morel, get your gear and we'll get organized."

"Thanks, Baby, I look forward to this. I mean, they told me you were hot and all and when I was told I was gonna be under some hot chick named Baby, I got a little--"

I didn't let him finish his sentence. I knew where this was going. I punched him and didn't pull it like I usually do.

"Been awhile since you did that," Romeo drawled as he walked over and looked at the soldier who was out cold on the sidewalk.

"Too long," I sighed and stepped over Morel to find the asshole in charge.

TWELVE

PTSD SPECIAL

BABY

Morel decided he would be better served following Romeo into battle. It was a wise decision on his part, probably the first he had made in a long time.

This left me teamed up with Heather Murphey and a few troopers that were on her team. This was fine by me. Murphey was actually an old friend of mine and the reason we had hooked up with this group in the first place. She came looking for me and the MJ group for reinforcements to help take out Lakeview. And I guess the rest is history.

We loaded up the vehicle with more weapons and supplies and opened up the roof rack. It was equipped with a defensive kit, so the roof folded up and out so a shooter could use the roof plates for cover. There would be four fighters in the vehicle, and the rest of the team would be mounted on four-wheelers and bikes that they'd gathered in the last week.

"We're going in at two in the morning, that's in six hours, people. Get some rest," Poche called after we gathered in the front room of the mansion they had taken over. All the vehicles were ready, everything was locked and loaded, we all had our orders - it was now a waiting game.

"You and Lani can crash in my room," Murphey said and motioned for us to follow her. She had a room on the first floor to the back of the house. It was down a hallway, past the kitchen and breakfast bar, so most likely where a full-time servant had lived, but the room was large and carpeted, which was perfect. I threw my pack down on the ground and sprawled out.

Lani tried to do the same, but it was obvious she wasn't used to sleeping on a hard floor. She couldn't hold still. She squirmed and sighed until Murphey relented.

"Shit. Take the bed," she grumbled and yanked her blanket off and threw it down on the floor by me.

"I can sleep on the floor, I'm fine," Lani whined.

"Just take the bed, Lani, Murphey and I are used to sleeping on the ground," I tried to reassure her but her frown in the dim room told me I had done the opposite.

"I know you guys think I'm soft, but I'm not, I can handle this," she said but her voice was high-pitched and whiny not sounding capable, only child-like. I knew exactly how she felt. My first two years in the military were a constant battle against men and other women who thought because of my size, how I looked, and my voice, that I couldn't do the job. It wasn't until my first tour, even after going through Ranger school, that I finally began to earn the respect I deserved. It wasn't until after I had taken out nearly a dozen enemy combatants in one of the most horrendous fire fights I'd ever experienced that I became one of the "guys." I still had nightmares about that day. I didn't want Lani to have to go through something like that.

"I think it's more that we want you to be soft, or to stay soft," I argued.

"That's unfair. I don't want to be soft, soft people die. You and Romeo think you're protecting me by shielding me, but I don't want to be shielded."

"Give it time, Lani, you'll be as fucked as the rest of us," Murphey yawned. "Might as well enjoy not having PTSD while you have the luxury." She laughed, her dark humor too close to the truth for comfort.

"Y'all aren't, fu–fucked," she stumbled over the curse word as if she wasn't used to it.

"Yeah we are, we just know how to hide it well. Get some rest, Lani, we have a neighborhood to invade and some bikers to kill, gotta be well-rested for that," Murphey joked again and Lani took the hint, throwing herself on the bed with a sigh.

I couldn't let myself slide over into sleep until both of their breaths evened out and I knew they were out.

THIRTEEN

GOING IN HOT

BABY

It was dark as fuck as I got into the back of the vehicle. We had one of the troopers driving, an older man by the name of Nigel. He had his partner in the passenger seat and Murphey and I took the backseat. We were packing M4s and had them converted to fully automatic.

We were going in guns blazing.

We were flanked on both sides by two crotch rockets, with modified mufflers to suppress the sound, and one four-wheeler. They had mounted a rifle on the handle bars of the four-wheeler with a shit-ton of duct tape. It looked ridiculous and dangerous. If that came loose, he could do some serious damage to himself or the soldiers around him. Glad I wasn't on that post.

"We're going in hard and fast. Team One is going up Robert E. Lee and taking out the watch at the Orleans Canal, Team Two is going up Filmore and taking out that watch there. Three is coming up the rear behind One after they take out the first watch, and Four is coming up from the Jefferson side and taking out the watch at Bucktown," Poche reiterated the plan we had gone over a million times.

Team One was Zach and Blake's team, Team Two was Romeo's team and ours was Three. There was a fifth team which was basically clean-up and manned by the civilians and Poche who was acting as our Napoleon. Isaiah, our compound's doctor, and Lani were also in the fifth team, their job was to help secure the females and children. They wouldn't come in until we gave them an all-clear and were ready to go in and get the hostages.

Nigel started the vehicle and we pulled out, following closely behind Blake's vehicle. We weren't using headlights, we wanted to surprise them.

We pulled onto the main street that would take us into Lakeview. The street was a two-lane expanse separated by a wide neutral ground with overhanging trees that were being overtaken by bush killer vines. There was a full moon tonight but the area was still pitch black and I could barely make out anything in front of us. The anxiety from not being able to see had my palms sweating.

Nigel and Blake, the drivers, were sporting night vision, so they could see where they were going. The rest of us were blind.

After a few moments I noticed a glow in the distance. It was the bikers stationed at the Orleans Canal floodgate. Our intel told us it would be two of them. They were using road blocks, nothing more than large plastic bins filled with sand and water, to stop people from plowing through.

We neared the canal and the glow became brighter and I could make out the shapes in the distance. We were at an advantage, we could see them, but they couldn't see us, blinded by the light of a campfire they had started. They had also parked their trucks close and were using the headlights to illuminate their area, instead of the area around them. It was a novice move, but it showed they were more worried about zombies than a human attack.

Nigel pulled off his goggles as one of the men stood up in the first vehicle, it looked like Zach. The sound of our engines had the bikers jumping to their feet and raising their guns, peering into the darkness, but unable to see anything.

"Party's over gentleman, hands in the air and come out slowly," Zach called. The biker closest to us raised his gun and fired.

Zach didn't flinch, he opened fired and two bodies fell to the ground, as our vehicle came to a stop.

Far off in the distance I heard another burst of gunfire. Another team had taken out an entry point.

The bikes came screaming around us, their sound muffled, but not enough for stealth. The riders jumped off and went straight to the road blocks. It took two men to move the water-filled impediments, but they got them out of the way and were back on their bikes in seconds.

Team One clicked on their high beams and tore into Lakeview, our vehicle close on their tail. They would know we were coming now, alerted by the gunfire and the sound of the bikes. There were no surprises from here on out. We were going in hot, how I liked it.

FOURTEEN

SHOTGUN MORNING

REBEL

An explosion of gunfire had me shooting up to a sitting position and reaching for my piece. Two more shots and I was surging to my feet and yanking on my boots. I had gotten into the habit of going to bed in my jeans and at least a t-shirt since this whole end of the world thing. Couldn't be caught with your pants down, you might trip, fall on your face and get bit.

It took a moment to orient myself. My head was throbbing for some reason and I still wasn't used to being in the gym with the kids. I had to stop and take a deep breath before I took a step. My positioning was off, but soon my inner compass kicked in and I realized where I was and where the shots had come from. I found a bottle of water on my make-shift nightstand, and I guzzled it down. My throat was on fire like I had slept with my mouth open and it had dried out.

Another round of gunfire rocketed through the air, it was loud and close. It was coming from Robert E. Lee. I heard the children crying and the sound of small feet heading in my direction, fast.

"Rebel, something's happening," one of the younger kids, Tina, an eight year old, whined at the entrance of my sleeping area.

"Come here," I said and exited my berth. I pulled her close to me and reassured her by holding her hand.

"Let's all get behind the counter, get down and stay quiet," I shouted. More little feet on the carpet came toward me. It was dark in here, only one lantern was still lit, but it was on the counter I wanted them to hide behind. It would be easy for them to find their way.

The sniffles of a child crying had me gritting my teeth. I had no idea what was going on. *Were we under attack by the biters?* Or by humans? There was no way to know, unless I went outside. I couldn't go outside. I couldn't leave the children. I was in charge and no one was going to come in and relieve me. If I left there would be no one here to watch them.

I didn't enjoy my new job, but I couldn't walk out on the little brats.

I stood on the other side of the counter, with my gun at the ready, trying to peer through the front glass windows. It was so damn dark, but there was a bright light coming from behind the front building. The glass of the offices on the second and third floors shone like a light bulb. I couldn't see a thing, though. Felicity, with her new, close-cropped hair looked over at me with big scared eyes.

"What's going on?" she said, her voice quavering from fear.

"I don't know," I said honestly. Her answering whimper made me regret that answer. I had to find out what was going on. I had to get us to safety.

"I'll find out. Stay here, keep the younger kids safe. I'll be right back." I left her and the rest of the children and went to the back door where a guard was supposed to be posted. The door led to a back parking lot that wasn't secured, so this door should be guarded at all times. Should be.

I knocked on the door and called out, but no one answered. There was no one guarding the door. I tried to open it, but it was locked. It wasn't reinforced; I could probably kick it open. But I didn't know what would be on the other side. I needed to be informed.

I turned and ran to the other side of the building, to the front glass doors. These doors usually were guarded too, but the guard was missing. The front door was glass and left unlocked, so I walked out into the yard and noticed a good amount of the men were running toward the front gate. I grabbed one of civilians as he ran past me from the men's quarters.

"What's going on?" I asked him.

"I don't know, I think we're under attack," he yelled and pulled out of my grasp to take off again.

"By who or what?"

"An army!" he called back and he didn't look scared, he looked excited.

FIFTEEN

SHOOT TO KILL

BABY

I held on as the vehicle powered through the crumbling streets of Lakeview. This was an all-terrain vehicle so it wasn't an issue, but it did throw you around a lot. The roar of the engines and the screaming of the bikes that surrounded us had my adrenaline jacked up. This was what I lived for. This was it. This was war.

The lead vehicles squealed into the parking lot of the strip mall, fishtailing and shining their lights on figures rushing from the building.

"Morning, boys!" I laughed a bit maniacally.

There was no "stop or we'll shoot," or announcement of who we were. Zach opened fire on the armed men from his position on the roof. They dropped in the street, their guns useless. They hadn't even fired. Three down.

Our vehicle screamed to a stop and Murphey and I used the roof shield and pointed the M4s at the door. The soldiers and troopers on bikes jumped off them and took cover behind the doors of the bigger vehicles.

Now it was time to let them know who was here. Who was going to kick their ass.

The third vehicle rolled in carrying Poche and the civilians. He got out of his vehicle, fully visible in his uniform, and raised a bullhorn. When he had taken the third vehicle I thought he was being a typical officer and leading from the rear. But he was the most vulnerable of us right now. My respect went up.

"Southern Clan, this is the United States Army, you are surrounded. You will come out now and give yourself up, or we will come in and take control, by force."

An unnatural silence settled over the area.

I could almost hear Murphey's heartbeat.

Three shots rang out. Crack. Crack. Crack. I saw the flash of a muzzle, high and to the south. The shots came from above us and in what felt like slow motion one of the troopers fell. I thought they would try to take out Poche, but they had gone for a trooper who had been trying to take cover behind the four-wheeler. It was a head shot, their sniper was a good shot.

"Sniper. On the roof," I called into my communication.

"Get ready to go in," my com buzzed with Blake's voice.

"I'm going up there to take out the sniper," Romeo's voice crackled through the com.

"Roger," Blake replied. "Cover Romeo, I need Chaillot with him. Then we'll breach the main building. Just like we planned, people. We've got these assholes. Only take prisoners if they've got two hands in the air or their dirty faces pressed in the ground at your feet. If not, shoot to kill."

SIXTEEN

TAKING CHANCES

REBEL

The squeal of tires and a sudden burst of headlights shone across the yard, illuminating the civilians as they gaped through the chain-link fence. These vehicles were coming from the Jefferson side of the base. We were getting overrun from both sides. *Who was in the vehicles? Was it us or someone else?* I couldn't tell. I wanted to go to the fence to see what was going on, but the children were more important. If it was a horde of biters, or something else, this supposed army, I was the only one armed that could protect them.

A hail of gunfire exploded and I fell back and crouched low.

Those weren't our guns.

"Southern Clan, this is the United States Army, you are surrounded. You will come out now and give yourself up, or we will come in there and take control, by force."

I turned and ran back to the gym, almost falling into the room as I pushed the glass doors open and ran across the slick tile.

"Tennis shoes, pants and jackets on now, kids!" I shouted from the center of the large area. Heads popped up from behind the counter. It was dark, but from the lantern that burned low, I could see the fear in their eyes. If it was the Army, they wouldn't attack the children, but I doubted this was the actual Army. If the United States Army was still functioning we would have heard something. We would have seen some sign of them. *Right?*

"Hurry up," I urged them with my hands. "Nick, Felicity and Pete, help the younger ones, we have to move fast." We were going to get out of here. In this room we were sitting ducks. If they came in and shot first, we could all be killed. I had to make sure the kids were in a safe place. The Clan wouldn't give up easily. It was going to be a bloodbath.

Sure enough, the sound of gunfire exploded through the air. I didn't know what side had fired, but it meant the Clan hadn't surrendered.

The kids were quicker than I expected. In under five minutes they were in front of me dressed in warm clothes and tennis shoes. Some of them clutched little bags, the older kids had packs on their back. I had grabbed mine, stuffed with the food I had been stashing. If this succeeded and we got out, it wouldn't be only me now. It would be me and eighteen kids. I didn't want to think about those implications.

I led them to the back door and held my hand up for them to wait. I went to the door and kicked it hard. The door shook, but held. I kicked it again and it still held. Two more kicks and the door shook in its frame and finally busted open. It was early morning, maybe four or five. The sun had not risen over the horizon, only a slight lightening of the sky indicated it was in the early hours of morning.

The crack of gunfire ricocheted through the air again. It was the clackety, clackety, clack of automatic gun fire. I knew the Clan didn't have automatic weapons. The most we had were a couple of rifles from the National Guardsmen, which could only shoot semi-automatic fire. This was a bigger, deadlier sound.

"We're going to run across the parking lot into the houses across the street," I said in a low voice, loud enough so all the kids could hear.

"We'll hole up in the houses until it's all clear," I said. "Then we'll find a safe place, okay?" Their small heads nodded.

"What about my mommy?" Tina, the youngest, sniffled.

"Your mom will be fine, it's the Army, they protect women and children," I said to reassure them. I hoped to God it was true. But it made me pause. What about the women? I was going to take their children into the unknown. Leaving could put everyone at risk. *Was it a chance I was willing to take?*

SEVENTEEN

DOWN GIRL

BABY

Shots rang out again as Romeo raced across the parking lot to the access ladder on the side of the building. I fired suppressive fire in the direction of the roof where I had seen the telltale flash of muzzle fire. Romeo and Chaillot were quick. They crossed the lot and were climbing the side of the building in a flash. The two were dressed from head to toe in black, and Romeo pulled his mask into place before he went in, so all you saw were his eyes.

Gun fire erupted the moment he threw his leg over the side of the roof and I held my breath and fired in the direction of the shooter again. I couldn't spot the sniper, so my firing was to make the shooter take cover.

Two more shots and then Romeo's voice over the com, "Shooter is down."

"Good job, we're going in. Drouet and Lambert, get up to the roof with Romeo. Find the access hole into the women's room and go in that way," Poche ordered.

Team One raced across the parking lot, Blake in the lead. They spread out around the door and then motioned for our team to follow them in. I ran across the parking lot and joined my team as we fell into a half circle pattern around the door. I pulled my mask down over my face and adjusted my weapon. I would be switching to a handgun if things got dicey inside, but right now I needed the rifle.

"One, two..." Zach's voice counted over the com and in real life. On three, I emptied a few rounds into the glass door and it shattered. As the door crashed down into a million pieces, I fell back out of the line of fire.

Shots erupted from inside. They were firing at us.

Zach threw a tear gas canister through the door. From the plans Lex had drawn, this door opened to a long corridor that ascended upward into the main room. The corridor was surrounded by high walls and had a steep grade. The bikers would be able to fire down on us, it could be deadly.

Gun shots erupted again, but I heard a few distinctive coughs and gags coming from inside the room. Zach followed up the tear gas with a flash bang. With our goggles and masks in place we were immune to it. We entered the building ready to shoot anything that moved.

Everything slowed down as we crossed the threshold. The room was filled with smoke, a few bikers were in the corridor coughing, their eyes tearing up from the gas, but they still raised their weapons as we ascended into the building. I made sure to flank Alexis who insisted on going in with all of us. She and Duke were the only non-military or police allowed on the frontline. Duke would be coming in with Ito from the West side of the complex, so all I had to worry about was Lex.

The place was dark and rancid. I fired at the first biker I saw, his hand was raised to fire. He fell and I rushed to his side and planted one in his forehead. Just in case.

The next biker I found took one look at me, dropped his weapon and raised his hands into the air.

"I give up!" he choked out. His face was aflame and snot poured out of his nose. I pushed him to his knees, keeping my gun trained on him as I pulled out zip ties and restrained him at the wrists and ankles. Poche had a large stock of the double restraint zip ties that the MPs liked to use. It made my job much easier.

Once I had him on his side and fully restrained, I patted him down, taking all of his weapons and depositing them in my pockets. When I was satisfied he was harmless, I stood up, paranoid over how exposed I had been during this takedown. This could have been a trap.

"You can't leave me like this," he called as I stepped over him.

"Fuck you," I called back.

Four more dead bikers lay in my path as I pushed deeper into the dark room. I switched the torch on my rifle on; the room was dark and filled with smoke. The bikers had cut all the lights to give them the advantage.

Something hit me hard from the side when I crested the landing into the main room. A biker had been hiding behind some shelving. He was a big fucker and I went down under him. He rose up, a knife in his hand, and attacked. I had to drop my M4. It clattered across the floor and the light went out suddenly, plunging us into darkness. I used my small size to my advantage, and hit him hard with my forearm. It connected with his nose and there was the nice sound of crunching cartilage.

He grunted and fell to the side slightly, enough that I could bring my knee up to my chest, more space between our bodies was a good thing. I dragged my combat boot down his leg and then brought it up hard into his dick. He screamed like a fucking girl and I got out from under him. I drew and fired in one quick motion. I hit him in the leg. Enough to hurt, but not to take him down.

I fired and hit him again in the shoulder, and this time he fell back. I scrambled to my feet and took him out with a shot to the head. I didn't see my M4 anywhere, so I went on without it. I couldn't waste time. I had plenty of clips for my nine, but I was now without a light.

I saw another light in the distance and followed it. When I caught up to it, I saw it was Lex. She was standing over a biker and kicking the shit out of him.

"Where the fuck is Junior? He hiding in the back like the fucking pussy he is?" she yelled.

"Lex," I said and I touched her arm. She spun on me, and her eyes were crazy in the light of her torch, her cheeks flushed from the adrenaline. "Down, girl," I said quietly.

"Fuck you, you cunt bitch," the man at our feet spat and surged to his feet. He pulled a gun from his boot. Lex must not have patted him down. I fired and took him out before he could use his weapon. He didn't have his hands up, or his face planted at my feet. Oops.

"I need to find Junior," she said to me.

"We'll find him, come on." I pulled at Alexis and we went deeper into the shit. I smelled smoke. Something was burning and that wasn't good. If they burned this place to the ground while we were in it, we'd all be fucked.

EIGHTTEEN

DO OR DIE

REBEL

It sounded like a war zone outside. Gun fire was a constant background noise. A lot of it was coming from the parking lot I needed to get these kids to cross. I was torn. We couldn't stay here, but we couldn't leave.

If we left the safety of this room, we ran the risk of running into whoever was firing on the place, or one of the bikers who would view our leaving as treason.

I made a split decision and pushed the door wide. Poking my head out, I saw nothing in the parking lot. It was time to go.

"Let's get out of here." I held the door open and motioned for the older kids to go out first.

"Across the lot to the big yellow house. Fast, now," I said in a low voice, but loud enough so all the kids could hear.

"Tina, come here." She was the littlest, so I moved my pack in front of me and bent down so she could climb onto my back. "Hold on to my straps. I can't hold on to you, I'll need my hands free," I said.

It was a do or die situation. Time to get the hell out of here.

NINETEEN

BEING CIVILIZED

BABY

Alexis and I took out four more targets and I had two more in zip ties and on the floor in a matter of minutes. I left the bikers that surrendered on the filthy floor in the dark, not caring about their fate. They deserved what they got, even if they did give up, there was no question about it. We had the back and front entrances guarded, this was probably the safest place for them.

"Area one is clear," Blake's voice came over the com.

"What about two?" Alexis asked, referring to the former coffee shop and the leader's room which was located at the west side of the big building.

"We're going in now," Zach answered. Alexis took off running across the room, skidding to a stop when she neared a group of shelving set up for the sleeping berths.

"The main area is right around this berth," she said in a whisper to me as I approached. We both held our guns tight to our bodies and rounded the corner, on alert. Zach and Blake were already there with another trooper I didn't recognize. Blake motioned for us to stay back, but Alexis wasn't having any of it. She shook her head and pointed at the door to the room that was once an employee only area. It was surrounded by a high counter littered with alcohol bottles and beer cans.

"He's gotta be in there," she whispered over the com. "I'm going in there to get the scumbag."

Blake looked pissed and he held his hand up for her to wait and get down. We used the counter as cover and crept closer to the room.

"I'm going in first," Blake whispered and I could see Lex's shoulders tighten in frustration. I think she really wanted to go in there guns blazing, but Blake was trained for this and she wasn't. No matter how much life experience Lex had clocked in her time in this post-Z world it wouldn't come close to what Blake and Zach had racked in their time in the Sandpit.

The room had three large glass panels covered with thick make-shift curtains along the front of the room. Blake moved to the side of the windows and motioned for Zach to take the other side. Lex and I held back, we would be needed soon.

Blake raised his weapon and fired two shots into the glass window. The safety glass came tinkling down to the floor in a crunchy waterfall of tiny shards. We went low after Blake's shot, taking cover as a barrage of shots fired from inside the room.

There was someone in there hiding. *Score.*

Zach stood and fired into the room again, not seeing a target, only firing for effect.

"Come out now, you're surrounded. We can stay here all day, can you?" Blake called.

"Fuck you!" a gravelly voice shouted from inside the room.

"Oh c'mon, is that you, Junior? Don't you want to come out and play with me." Alexis stood and I grabbed her leg to pull her down again. *Crazy girl!*

"I knew you'd be back, ya slut. Should have taken you from the old man and fucked you properly. Then none of this shit would be going down," he called, and I could hear the smile in his voice. The fucker was enjoying this.

Blake wasn't.

Blake threw a flash bang into the room and everything exploded in light and sound. The men were quick. They didn't even bother with the stairs, they jumped up the three feet through the broken glass and were in the room hollering at Junior before I had moved from my position.

Lex and I followed. She rushed in while I covered our backs.

Blake and Zach were screaming at a man, who was pushed into a corner. He was gripping a revolver in shaking hands. He pointed it at Zach and Blake but his eyes were blinking rapidly and tearing. He probably couldn't see much.

"Put the fucking gun down!" Blake screamed.

"Shoot the motherfucker!" Lex screamed.

The gun dropped to the man's feet and Lex surged forward with her gun cocked and ready. I grabbed for her and she violently shrugged me off, but it aided in slowing her down.

"Lex, stand down!" I yelled at her. She turned, her shoulders slumped, and she gave me an apologetic look.

Zach was already on the man, pushing him to his stomach and holding his M4 to the man's head.

"Are you the leader, the one called Junior?" Zach asked, his voice even and restrained.

"Fuck you," the man said, his voice muffled from being pressed into the dirty carpet.

"That's him," Lex said, walking closer to the man. "How'd ya like the present I left you when I escaped, Junior? Did your daddy turn? It's something I've been wondering since Z started. Do all the dead turn, or do you have to be bitten? What happened, Junior? Was daddy a zombie when you found the mess I left you?"

"My father was weak, an addict, I should have taken over a long time ago. I would have fucked you so hard you wouldn't have been able to move, much less escape."

Zach kicked him in the ribs and he hissed out a muffled cry. He must want to die. Or he was that cocky. I found my finger moving to my trigger. I shouldn't have stopped Lex.

Lex motioned for Zach to step away. I was surprised when he stepped back to the wall. Alexis walked to Junior and stuck a foot under him. She turned him over with a hard kick of her booted foot. When he was on his back and looking up at her, she stepped forward and pressed down on his stomach with her foot, making him wince.

"I knew you wanted more," he smiled, his lips bloody from the take-down.

"I did come back for more, but this time you'll be the one on the bottom." She kicked out, a hard slam into his ribs. Junior gasped and curled into a fetal position.

"I can't wait, cunt," he managed to spit out.

I looked up in time to see Zach raising his weapon. He cocked it, but Blake yelled something to stop him. Zach looked at his friend but continued to raise his gun.

I wanted this worthless piece of shit eradicated from the planet too, but Poche wanted this one in particular left alive and technically he was on his back, at our feet. Shooting a man, unarmed and broken at our feet, wasn't how you did things. Our world might be shit, this guy might be the worst of the worst, but, we had a plan and that plan was to handle this civilized, like. If they surrendered, if they were down, we were taking them prisoner.

You didn't shoot helpless men.

Blake surged across the room and gripped Zach's wrist. He was too slow, though. The gun fired and the bullet slammed into the floor only a few feet from Junior. In this tiny room, the explosion from the gun was deafening. My ears began to ring as the last of the sound faded away.

The whole world had slowed down again. The flickering of one lantern in the corner was our only light besides the flashlights on the ends of some of our rifles. Blake held Zach back, his arms around him, saying something to him that I couldn't make out because my ears were still ringing with the echoes of the shot. Zach's eyes were wide and crazed and focused on the man on the floor. The gun still gripped in his hand.

Junior was a nothing of a man. He lay there, on his back, bloody, but he still had a smile on his face. The motherfucker was enjoying this. This punk kid, dressed up like a biker, dirty and unkept, had caused quite a shitstorm.

Lex pushed between the two men and placed her hands on Zach's face to make him focus on her. Blake was still talking Zach down as Zach looked from Lex to Blake and back again. Lex managed to free the gun from Zach's tight grip and then pulled him into a tight embrace.

I looked at the man who lay on his back between us, the cause of all this drama. He didn't look like much. How had someone like this done so much damage? In any other situation he would be your average guy. There was something wrong with him, though, something off. In the midst of this craziness he lay there, staring up at all of us as if he didn't have a care in the world, as if we were entertainment. He looked back and forth between us like this was just another day for him.

When he began to laugh, drawing the attention of the trio still fighting for control in the corner, I had had enough. I bent down, grabbed him by his shirt and punched him hard in the face. He slumped, unconscious in my grip. I let him fall to the floor, not caring about his head slamming into the hard linoleum. *That solved that problem.*

TWENTY

AWOL KIDDIES

My com buzzed with static and I was surprised I could hear it since there was still a low ringing in my ears.

"We have area three secured. The women are being evacuated," a voice I didn't recognize came over our communication.

"Ito, check in area five?" Poche's voice asked.

"Area now secured, sir. We're moving in on area four. Male civilians have not been evacuated," Ito replied after a short pause.

I walked out of the small room, leaving Blake, Zach and Alexis alone to calm down. I could relate to what Lex was going through. She had never told me what had happened here, but the fucker on the floor had made it pretty clear.

There was no worse feeling.

The feeling of being helpless. Someone stronger having control over you, controlling you in every way, even sexually, was soul-shattering. Especially if that person had no concern about your well-being.

I had decided a long time ago that it would never happen to me, again. If you could think it, I had experienced it when I was neck deep in the foster care system. Nightmare after nightmare, until I had finally had enough and learned how to defend myself. It pained me that Lex had experienced this. But she was strong, she wouldn't let it rip her apart. And it helped that she had killed one of her abusers and had the other one at her feet. I never had that satisfaction.

"I need a status on area four," Poche's voice again in my ear.

"Area four is deserted, sir, the children are gone," Murphey answered. She must have broken off from the main area and joined up with Ito.

"What do you mean, gone?" Poche asked.

"Gone. No one is here. Back door is open." I could hear the exasperation in Murphey's voice.

"Shit, we need to find them. Someone could have taken them, or they're out there alone. I need trackers on them, stat," Poche responded, his professional radio voice gone.

"Murphey, I'll meet you in the back lot, we'll find them," I spoke into the com.

"Are y'all good in here?" I asked as the trio came out of the small room, Zach dragging Junior behind him.

"Yeah, we're gonna round up all the prisoners and secure them," Blake said, placing his gun down on the counter and digging out a bigger torch from his pack.

"Call in five to do clean-up, they were dying to get in on the action," I smirked and Lex rolled her eyes, but she returned my smile.

"Go find those kids," she said and motioned for me to leave. She didn't have to tell me twice. That's all we needed was some stupid biker holding a bunch of kids hostage.

TWENTY-ONE

EMPTY JUNK DRAWERS

REBEL

It took forever to make it across the lot. The gunfire had stopped, but I wasn't taking chances. I hurried the children as fast as I could, but some were slow and all of them were scared.

When we made it to the first house, I noticed the door had been kicked in. We couldn't stay there if the house wasn't secure. I moved them further into the neighborhood, but it looked like the same fool had done it to all the houses in the area. I would have to use a board or something to secure the door.

I made a split second decision and had them enter one of the larger houses on the block. I would have to deal with the door later.

"C'mon kids, hurry." I motioned for them to enter. "Nick and Pete, take the lead just in case." Nick had a bat and Pete was carrying what looked like a tire iron. They nodded and went in fast while I fell to the back of the group and made sure all the kids entered, counting off each of them. I wasn't concerned there would be any biters inside, we had cleared this area a long time ago.

When the final child ran into the house, I breathed a sigh of relief, which quickly led to fear as I heard the soft pound of footsteps coming my way. It was rhythmic, a fast run, not biters, but still scary as hell. They were coming fast in our direction and when I turned to face the base, I saw the flash of something in the distance. A flashlight. They were far enough away that they might not have seen me. I clicked off my light and rushed into the house.

I tried to secure the door behind me, but it was a lost cause. It was splintered in places and it hung from its hinges, loose and useless.

"Everyone upstairs. Nick, get them settled and quiet. Pete, I need you down here to help me lock down the house." The two boys nodded and got moving.

I went into the kitchen and clicked on my flashlight again. I tried to keep it low so it wouldn't throw off any light and draw unwanted attention. Most people kept a tool box or at least a hammer in a junk drawer in the kitchen, so I began to search drawers.

The drawers turned up nothing but old receipts and used birthday candles. I went to the side door, hoping for a laundry room, but got a pantry instead. I shined the light near the bottom and something scurried across the shelves.

I jumped back, knocking something over in the process. From the smell, it was vinegar. I shined my light across the floor again, revealing a good sized rat and breathed a sigh of relief. Nothing dangerous.

"Hands-up, fuckface," a hard voice said behind me.

I hadn't heard a thing, not a door open or the creak of the floor. And now my lack of awareness was going to get me killed.

TWENTY-TWO

MORONS AND MIGRAINES

BABY

It wasn't hard to find the fool that had taken the kids. He ran out the back door and went to the biggest house. I don't know what his plans had been. I couldn't even begin to imagine because I don't think like a criminal pedophile, but it was going to be an easy takedown.

Murphey and I stood in front of the house we had seen the kids enter. We stayed hidden behind the thick foliage that was once a garden. I signaled for her to enter through the front and she nodded. I went around the side, staying low and quiet. The house was nothing but windows, I could see into it easily. When I got to the back, I noticed the muted glow of a light.

I went into stealth mode, taking a deep breath and centering myself, aware of everything around me. There was a backdoor that led to the kitchen and it was standing ajar, the lock broken and useless.

He didn't look up when my boot squeaked on the tile floor. He was too busy digging through the pantry, making a racket in his haste to find what he was looking for. He only noticed me when I was right on top of him and started to order him around.

Not much of a criminal mastermind if you ask me.

"Are you fucking deaf, I said hands-up." His hands shot into the air and he turned around to face me. He was younger than I expected. And not as scruffy as the rest of the group. His beard was thick, but neat, and he looked trim under the leather jacket he wore, very trim actually. He was also attractive with dark blond hair, close cropped to his head, and dark eyes that shone with fear.

His hand didn't twitch for his piece which was shoved into his pants like an amateur. I holstered my own piece, keeping my torch trained on his eyes to blind him. I stepped forward and grabbed his gun from his waistband. My knuckles brushed against hard, fit muscles instead of the soft flesh I would have expected from a biker.

I checked the clip and pocketed the firearm. There was some kind of stench coming from this pantry, like bleach, or vinegar, or some other awful cleaning fluid. It was seeping into my brain and giving me a migraine. It was my only excuse for what came out of my mouth next.

"Got anything else down your pants?" I asked, thinking it would sound cocky, but it came out sounding flirtatious.

Well, this was a new one for me. It took everything in me not to shoot him right there so I wouldn't have a witness to my own stupidity.

TWENTY-THREE

FLIRTING WITH DISASTER

REBEL

I had expected some big Army guy when I turned around. What I saw when I pivoted to face the gruff orders was a small figure, not much bigger than Felicity. She had a soft, high-pitched, female voice that was in weird contrast with how she was dressed and her words. She might have been tiny, but she was dressed to kick ass. She was dressed for war. She was in all black fatigues with combat boots laced up tight and was even equipped with combat armor. Some of it looked homemade, but the majority looked high-tech.

Her face was covered in a mask and she was wearing goggles over her eyes. The only piece of skin I saw was the tips of her fingers wrapped around a handgun, and a rather lush set of lips.

Those fingers were tight around a handgun pointed confidently at me. She motioned with her gun in an upward motion. I raised my hands higher.

"I have a .22 and a knife in my boot," I said, answering her question.

"What the fuck is that smell?" She stepped back.

"I knocked over the vinegar," I said, trying not to let her hear the fear in my voice. I didn't know this girl's intentions. Was she here to kill me and the children? Was that the goal? Why else would she have come out here to find us? We weren't threatening anyone.

"Get out of the pantry and close the door. I can't take that smell."

She had me there. I could almost taste the vinegar, it was that pungent, but it wasn't high up on my list of issues at the moment. I stepped out of the pantry and closed the door behind me, keeping my hands in plain sight like you see on the cop shows. Didn't want any sudden moves with my trigger happy friend here.

"Why did you take the kids?" she asked.

"There were gunshots, it wasn't safe," I replied.

"You weren't planning on keeping them as hostages?"

"Why would I do that?"

"Because we took over your base, killed half of your men and took your leader hostage. Leverage, you know, what the bad guys normally do." She shrugged, which I barely noticed through her armor.

"You're the one with a gun pointed at me," I said gruffly. "Who's the bad guy?"

"And you're the one with the biker patches all over you. You know, the same biker gang that was keeping women locked up as sex slaves and manufacturing meth and fun things like that. Bad guy shit. C'mon turn around, I need to restrain you. Slowly get the rest of your weapons out and throw them to the other side of the room."

"It's a motorcycle club," I said on autopilot, but I pulled out my gun and knife, throwing them across the room like she told me.

"Yeah, and I'm a fucking Girl Scout," she laughed and yanked me forward by my wrists, wrapping a zip tie around them roughly and then patting me down, obviously not taking my word for it.

"Murphey, you found the kids?" She did something with her ear.

"They're all upstairs," I shared. She held up a hand as if to shush me.

"Come in Poche, kids are secure, we're not far from the main area, advise," the blonde said, touching her ear and then motioning with her gun for me to sit down at the table.

The way she held herself and her casual way of giving orders let me know she was used to giving orders and having them followed. Her bearing was rigid and she handled her weapon with ease. This wasn't someone who picked up a gun after the infection and became an apocalypse guru. She was obviously military. And from the gear she was holding, it was even more evident. Could this really be the Army?

If that was the case, I was fucked.

TWENTY-FOUR

BEAUTY PAGEANT MILITARY

BABY

"Stay where you are. When we get this base locked down and the prisoners secure, we'll bring you in. I don't want to risk transporting them in the dark," Poche gave the order.

"Roger," I said in response.

"What's your name?" I asked the biker.

"Rebel," he said. They all had those dumb street names, but they weren't a gang. Sure.

"Okay, *Rebel*. We're going to bunker down for a bit, and you're not going to give me any trouble, are you? You look like a smart guy. As a smart guy, you should pick up on the fact that I really want a reason to put a few rounds into you. Act up and I get that chance. So, ya gonna behave?" He glared at me, but nodded obediently.

"Good boy," I smiled. My mask was itching and there was no need for the protection so I pulled it off and threw it on the table. I pulled a lantern from my pack, set it on the counter and turned it on. The was a clatter in the hallway and I spun around with my gun raised.

"You got someone else with you, Rebel?" I called over my shoulder.

"No, just the kids, it might be one of the kids." His voice was high and worried. He was truly scared that it was one of the kids. It made me second-guess my assumptions about him.

I holstered my gun, but kept it unclipped, at the ready. I palmed my knife, just in case it wasn't a living person. I crept through the kitchen and went to the large archway that led to the front of the house.

I noticed the slight shiver of a shadow in a recessed area and I moved through the doorway quickly, avoiding something that was swung near my face by only inches. I executed a quick turn and blocked the next attack. I grabbed the tire iron that was again aimed at my head. I disarmed the attacker with one quick move and got him locked in an arm bar, bringing him down to his knees. When he cried out in pain, I let up slightly. It wasn't a man's voice.

"You're kind of young for a biker, boy," I said through clenched teeth. He was obviously one of the kids, probably no older than fourteen.

"I ain't a biker," he cried out.

"Don't hurt him!" Rebel was in the doorway, his hands still tied in front of him.

I released the kid's arm and let him stand up straight. He rubbed at his arm and looked from me to Rebel.

"We're here to rescue you," I said and handed him back his tire iron.

"You with the military? You don't look like you're with the military," the kid said.

"Yeah, I'm with the military. The Guard wants their base back," I said. I looked up as Murphey came down the stairs and rounded the corner to take in the scene. She had also removed her mask.

"One of the older teens, Felicity I think, is getting the children to lay down while we wait this one out. There's an older boy, Pete, who wants to stand guard. They're a well-behaved bunch, but look a little shaken," Murphey reported as she took her M4 off and laid it on the dining room table within reach. The rifle was bulky, so I understood why she wanted it off, but I didn't trust this guy, no matter how docile he was acting.

"Rebel, I want you in this chair and don't even think about moving." I pushed a dining room chair up against the wall and gestured for him to sit down.

He was obedient and he wasn't even glaring anymore. He looked back and forth between me and Murphey.

"Is she military too?" Pete asked.

"Yup, anyone with me is military, well, most. We have a doctor and one of the women the bikers were keeping locked up. She wanted a little bit of payback." I made a point of looking at Rebel, who looked at his lap in response.

"What kind of military are you two? Is it like some kind of beauty pageant military?" I counted to ten, and turned it to twenty when I heard Rebel snicker.

"Trust me, kid," Murphey said in her toughest voice, which was much better than mine, at least she wasn't squeaky. "Don't say anything like that again."

TWENTY-FIVE

NOT IN FRONT OF THE KIDS

REBEL

It was hard to see their facial expressions from my position and the lantern light that threw shadows back and forth but I could gauge from the women's responses that Pete needed to shut up quick. He wasn't far off, though. The two female soldiers were attractive. The one that had been upstairs was tall and well-built, but she had soft features with big eyes and pretty honey-colored hair that fell down her back in a pony-tail.

Her counter-part, the prickly one that had tied me up, was the opposite. She was short, could be mistaken for a teen herself, with the whitest of blonde hair that's usually only seen on children. The only way I could describe her was cute, even though everything that came out of her mouth was the furthest from cute.

"How about you come sit by me, Pete," I said to stop the conversation before he put his foot in his mouth. I wasn't used to females like this. The ones that flocked around the MC were flaky and loose and willing to do about anything to get you to like them.

The blonde touched her ear again and tersely said, "Roger."

She looked at me and said, "I'm Hannah Klink, this is Heather Murphey," she motioned to her counterpart, "We're commandeering your camp for the United States Army National Guard and the Louisiana State Troopers. You're now under arrest for human trafficking and multiple counts of assault, rape and the exploitation of juveniles. You will be remanded and placed in confinement until the Army figures out what to do with you. You do not have any rights, since we are still under Marshall Law. If we still had a Homeland Security, you would be thrown in a hole and never seen again." She sounded like she was reciting something she was told to say.

"What does that mean?" I asked. Was there still Marshall Law because there was a functioning government?

"It means, you do what we say," Heather Murphey cut in.

"No, I mean, yes, I will do as you say, but does that mean there's still a government? That I'm going to be held until we get the local government back up and running? Whose orders are you taking?"

"We're trying to establish contact with command," Heather Murphey said tersely and I felt the wash of disappointment fall over me. So, they were as clueless as we were. Just wandering around looking for guidance in this terrible world.

"So, you decided in the meantime to take over our base," it would be a good time to put my filter in effect, but it wasn't something I knew how to do.

"Yes, actually we did. We might have left you guys alone if you had laid off the kidnapping. You know that human trafficking thing I mentioned? And even then we were thinking about leaving you guys alone, until you decided to grab one of ours," the blonde, Hannah, spit back.

"Hey, Rebel had nothing to do with that, he's one of the good guys,"

Pete spoke up and I could have kissed the kid.

"Bullshit." Heather Murphey pointed at my chest. "Last time I checked those pretty, racist patches all over his jacket make him one of them. Men like you make me sick." She turned and strode to the front door, leaving me with a glaring, micro-Barbie who wanted to shoot me.

"I really..." *I deserved that.*

"Like, I said, I wouldn't mind shooting you, but I think it might upset the kids. So, sit back, relax and zip it up. In about an hour, we'll get you back to the base."

"I'm yours to command," I said and it came out a bit more flirty or sarcastic, than I intended. She frowned at me and looked at Pete who was staring at us not quite understanding what was going on.

"I'm sure you'll come to regret that statement," she said coldly and smirked at me. My gut tightened and suddenly I had a feeling that I really would. I was being held by the last remnants of the Army and they thought I was the big bad. Nothing good could come out of this.

TWENTY-SIX

MONSTERS AMONG US

BABY

I didn't know what to think about our captive. After our initial inter-action, he quieted up and leaned his head back and feigned sleep. I knew he was faking it because every now and again he would look up and check his surroundings.

He didn't strike me as a predator either, more of a victim than any-thing. He looked freaked out and he had shown real concern for the children, and Pete in particular. Pete didn't leave his side, like he also had an attachment to the young biker.

I didn't want to feel empathetic for this loser, but I felt like I was keep-ing a civilian captive, not an enemy combatant. And that didn't sit well with me.

When the sky began to lighten and the sun rose over the deserted neighborhood, I knew it was time to move.

"Poche, this is Klink, we're ready to move."

"Roger, Klink, there is no sign of any movement your way, bring them in. We're placing the children in their former sleeping area." It was

Tammi Ryan who gave the orders, instead of Poche. The dynamic duo.

"Got it," I said and walked to Pete and Rebel.

"We're moving. We're putting the kids back in their former sleeping area. Pete, can you run upstairs and get everyone ready to go?" Pete nodded and stood, stretching his tight muscles.

"What are you going to do with Rebel?" he asked, unafraid of pissing me off again.

"He'll be held in confinement indefinitely," I said coldly.

"Us too, are we going to be held?"

"No, you'll be reunited with your parents and then your parents will decide if they would like to stay or move on. No one but the men that controlled the camp will be held against their will."

Pete nodded and looked at Rebel with regret obvious in his eyes. Rebel shook his head at the boy and tilted it to the side, indicating for him to go upstairs. Again the feeling that he really did care for the kid took surface. But what did that matter? That didn't make him less of a rapist or less of an opportunist. Just another man looking to take advantage of the weak. It didn't matter if he was protective of the kids, that just made him less of a monster.

But, still a monster.

TWENTY-SEVEN

BLOOD STAINS

REBEL

Heather Murphey and Hannah Klink moved everyone out of the house with stark efficiency. The women were rigid and had a take-charge persona the kids fell into step with.

Hannah escorted me, while Heather led the group back to the base.

"Take the kids through the back door. I'll bring this one to the holding area," Hannah called to Heather. Heather nodded her head and we split off from the group.

"Where are you holding the prisoners?" I asked

"In the office space above the grocery," she said. The grocery my brothers had been using as the main area was located on the first floor of a small office building. It was only four stories high and made up of mostly reflective glass windows on the upper floors.

The National Guard had been using it as storage when we joined the camp, but not much more. You couldn't open the windows, so there was little ventilation and it had been extremely hot in the summer when we had taken over. From what I know, our group hadn't even given the space much thought since.

Hannah led me through the main area and I tried not to look at the blood splatters that were everywhere. It was a war zone. Bodies were being dragged out of the room as we walked in and I winced when I saw the body of my father being unceremoniously dragged out by a guy in fatigues.

I didn't have a lot of love for the man, but he was still my only relative. I halted abruptly, turning around to watch my father leave a red stain of blood on the terrazzo floor.

"Come on," Hannah said to me and pulled on my arm, but stopped short when she got a look at my face. I wonder what she saw there.

Did I look like I was in pain? Maybe grieving? I didn't know what I was feeling. Regret?

"Friend of yours?"

"My father," I said quietly.

"I'm–," she began as if to say the compulsory, I'm sorry. But she stopped herself short and shook her head.

"C'mon Rebel, let's get you situated so I can get the fuck out of here. This place gives me the creeps."

"My name's Reid." For some reason, I didn't want her to call me Rebel anymore.

"I like that better," she said quietly.

"Yeah, so do I."

TWENTY-EIGHT

LEFT TO ROT

REBEL

She brought me to the third floor and left me. The other members of her team had cleared the floor and the remaining brothers were locked in the offices that faced the street.

I was placed in a room with Eagle, Jazz and Bayou. I would have thought Eagle would have gone down fighting. He wasn't one to give in easily. If he was alive, Junior was probably alive.

"Rebel," Jazz said when they pushed me into the office. It was cleared out and the only thing in there was a bucket in the corner and a few piles of blankets in the middle.

"Jazz," I said casually, taking in his appearance. All three of them looked disheveled and they had blood stains on their jackets. Everyone's wrists were secured, Jazz's were in front like mine, Eagle had his uncomfortably secured from behind.

It was hot in here. I had expected it to be freezing, but for some reason it was ridiculously hot. It must be the body heat. I had my leather jacket on and I wanted it off bad, but I couldn't because of the wrist restraints.

I had lost track of the days and months, but I knew it was probably mid-February or maybe March, and New Orleans was still in the grips of winter. It wasn't supposed to be this hot.

"So, Rebel," Bayou drawled out my name, "Where were you when we got invaded by the fucking Army?"

"With the kids, where y'all put me." I was suddenly dizzy, I placed my palm on the wall to steady myself. My throat was killing me also. It had been hurting for a while, but I hadn't paid it much attention. Too much happening around me. I went to the wall and leaned on it, trying to look casual, but I probably looked like a fool.

"Gave up without a fight, did ya?" Eagle sneered.

"It was me and a fourteen year old, wasn't much of a fight," I coughed and continued to cough until my lungs hurt. This made my throat hurt worse.

"Fuck, brother, are you sick?" Jazz asked, real concern lacing his words.

"No, I'm fine," I replied, but I was lying. I hadn't noticed before, probably because of the adrenaline, but there was a slight ache deep in my bones and my vision felt like it was fading.

"You don't look fine," he responded. "Sit down, on the other side of the room though." He killed any compassion with that statement.

I did as told, but only because I really wanted to sit down. I slid down the wall and took a sitting position. It was the wall with the bucket, it would be disgusting later, but it would give me space for now. I didn't want my brothers crowding in on me.

I leaned my head back until it hit the wall. I closed my eyes. The adrenaline had drained from me, leaving me weak and tired. I would take a little nap and then I would be fine. That was the plan.

TWENTY-NINE

SEX GODS AND DUST MITES

BABY

"I'm sure y'all are ready to get back to your little island?" A young trooper was trying to make conversation as I waited for Blake and Zach to get back from whatever they were doing with Poche and Ryan.

I couldn't figure out if his tone was snide or jealous. I would assume snide. I always saw the worst in people.

I shrugged and yawned. I was too tired to make conversation, especially with pissy privates. To be honest, I was dying to get back to our compound. *Dying.* I hated being in Lakeview. I hated this base. It was disgusting and depressing and there was no running water, or power and the smell of the dead permeated the entire area. I also couldn't get the smell of vinegar out of my nose. At least at the compound it was isolated, we were right on the lake, so the air was fresh and there was always a wind blowing. I had taken it for granted, but now, in this place, where the rot of the dead hung over the area, I felt ill at ease and jumpy.

As I sat there, I could smell the fires that burned the bodies of the dead. It was like being near a crematorium. *Disgusting.*

I knew what was going on. I knew the reason Poche and Ryan had spirited away Blake and Zach the minute we had the base locked down. The four leaders were in serious negotiations– and I knew one of those points was keeping some of us here for protection, until they got their base in order and locked up tight. They were also most likely trying to keep the tactical vehicles we had poached, along with some of our weapons.

It was never enough.

All I knew was I wasn't staying here one more day. Nope.

"This place is a shithole, I can't wait to get back to our island," Lex accentuated the last part, obviously noticing the soldier's tone too. She yawned and glared at me, I guess my yawn was catching. We were sprawled on a sofa that had been brought up to the second floor, which was being used as a command center.

"We're gonna make it great though, Poche has some good ideas and we'll get solar panels, a few cisterns and this place will be just like home," the trooper said eagerly.

"Call me when that happens." I smiled, but it must not have been reassuring because he blanched. Oh man, I must look bad.

"Uh, yeah, sure." He stood up from his chair and hurried off.

"You always scare the innocent ones off," Lex yawned again and slumped down next to me putting her head on my shoulder.

"I didn't scare you away when we first met," I laughed.

"I was hardly innocent when we met," she laughed with me.

"Bullshit, you were this baby, following Blake around like he was a god."

"You're the Baby, not me, toots. And I was following Blake around like he was a sex-god, get it right, I got my priorities." I heard the smile in her voice and smiled back even though she used that damned name again.

"I really don't want to hear that, he's my boss." I tried to get comfortable, but the sofa was cloth and I was imagining all the bugs that had used it as a home in the months since Z hit. The brown fabric had seen better days. *I needed to get the fuck out of here.*

"So, you don't want to hear about how he does this thing with his tongue, he just–"

"Shut it." I pushed her off my shoulder and she fell away laughing.

"Y'all look sleep deprived," Zach said as he walked into the waiting room, Blake right behind him, followed by Poche. They all swaggered, it was funny, each one jockeying for alpha male status.

"I wouldn't mind finding a bed somewhere," I spoke up.

"Me too, but not for sleeping, was telling Baby about that thing Blake does with his–"

"Argh!" I threw my hands up to cut her off and was even more freaked out when I saw the three of them looking at each other with deep and annoying love eyes.

"Can we go back to the compound?" I whined.

"Not quite, we have to make sure this place is secure and then we can go back," Blake said and Poche clapped him on the back. "Wouldn't want to leave them vulnerable for attack."

"I really appreciate this, Miller. We couldn't have done this without you and your team."

"It's mutually beneficial to both of us. Having Lakeview back under control will help get this city back in order," Blake said all officer like.

A young soldier poked his head into the room and caught Poche's attention.

"What is it?" Poche asked.

"Sir, we seem to have a sick prisoner."

"Already? Are you sure, or is he faking to try and escape?"

"I'm pretty sure this is legit, sir, he's running a really high fever and he's unconscious."

"Shit, that's all we need, something infectious," Zach cursed.

"Well, we already have an infirmary set up for the wounded, guess we have our first non-combat patient," Poche sighed and pulled a walkie off his belt.

"Ryan, can you get someone with a stretcher up to the third floor. We have a sick prisoner, probably want to quarantine him too. Wouldn't want a bug getting around the camp."

"This just keeps getting better and better," I yawned again.

"Which prisoner is it and what room is he in?" Ryan asked over the walkie. Poche looked at the soldier.

"Street name, Rebel. He's in office 3G," the soldier said and Poche relayed the information to Ryan.

My gut tightened. I blamed it on being sleep deprived.

THIRTY

SOMEWHAT RESPONSIVE

REBEL

I woke up being jostled down the stairs. I was being hauled around by two guys in fatigues. It was dark and I was on something really uncomfortable. I tried to stay awake so I could figure out what the hell was going on, but I was so tired.

Again I came to, but this time I was on a cot and someone was poking at me and shining some kind of light in my eye. I tried to swat them away but my arms were heavy and unresponsive. I thought it was one of those dreams where I would try to defend myself from an attacker, but I felt like I was under water.

"Rebel, can you hear me?" It was a female's voice. I recognized the voice, but I couldn't place it.

I tried to say something, anything, but it sounded gurgled even to my ears.

"He's somewhat responsive. I'm worried it's in his lungs. I would normally do an X-ray to check," the female's voice said.

"Treat him as if it is in his lungs, it sounds like it, and you can't take any chances. Get some antibiotics in him and get him on a fluid drip," a male voice said.

"We're really gonna waste our medical supplies on him-" another male voice said.

"What if–,"the female started to say, but I was fading fast. I wanted to hold on, I knew there was something wrong with me and I wanted to know what was going on. But it took me fast and again I slipped into sleep.

THIRTY-ONE

THE GOOD GUY

BABY

"He's the one I brought in, the one with the kids." I looked at the unconscious biker. He looked so much younger asleep. We were in the makeshift infirmary that Melinda and Isaiah had put up quickly. I was curious about what this guy had, since I had spent a few hours with him, I didn't want to come down with anything if it was contagious.

"You mentioned he didn't fight you, no resistance?" Blake asked incredulously.

"Yeah, in fact the kids defended him, called him a good guy, but that's not saying much considering what they were dealing with. Lesser evil, that sort of thing". Poche and Blake stepped out of the infirmary and I followed, not wanting to get in the way of the doctor and his capable nurse.

"I don't want to waste precious resources on him. No one is making antibiotics anymore, we have to protect the supply we have. Use them only in an emergency and on patients that are most deserving of them, it's a common triage practice," Tammi Ryan said coldly. "So, we save this man, to only put him to death in a few short weeks? How is that logical?"

"He hasn't been found guilty yet, Tammi," Poche said softly. "Of all of them, there have only been two that the civilians have spoken positively about. Him and one called Jazz."

"He's not like the rest of them." Melinda shared as she stepped out of the infirmary tent, pulling off latex gloves and sticking them in her pockets. If anyone knew about these men it was Melinda. She had helped Lex escape from them and had spent months in their captivity before that.

"But, he's still one of them. I just can't trust anyone wearing one of those patches," Ryan said stubbornly.

"Just keep it in mind, before you start giving execution orders," Melinda said quietly but firmly.

"I want him under constant watch, I don't want him coming to and taking out one of my men," Ryan fired back. "And I don't want to waste medical supplies on someone undeserving!"

"Well, too late, I've already hooked him up to an antibiotic drip. You'll have to find some other person to kill," Melinda hissed.

"When he wakes up and takes out one of our men, or you, don't say I didn't warn you," Ryan's tone was hard.

"I'll guard him," I spoke up and almost instantly regretted it. *What the hell was I agreeing to do?*

"Fine, he's your problem." Ryan walked out and Poche followed.

"Thanks, Baby, I appreciate this," Melinda said and her eyes widened when she realized she used my nickname. I let it slide, I was getting soft.

THIRTY-TWO

I'M UP

REBEL

I was dreaming about my captor, the cute blonde that wanted to shoot me. We were in a hallway that never ended and we were trying to find our way out, but it was a pointless task. We ran and ran, forever it seemed, but we never reached the end.

"Stop," she screamed and I did as she ordered. I liked when she ordered me around, but I would never admit that. Only in a dream.

"This way." She took my hand and I followed her. We turned in a new direction and there was a door, *finally*.

My eyes sprung open and they were finally clear. I was in a tent, some large white tent and there were a few cots next to me. I looked to my right and noticed a guy I didn't know, probably from the Army group. He was sleeping and hooked up to an IV. There was a nasty looking bandage across his face with a red blood stain seeping through it.

I was obviously in a makeshift hospital, most likely still at the base. I had been sick. I remembered the fever, I had been burning up and dizzy.

"Oh, you're up." A familiar face came into view.

"Melinda," I croaked.

"Rebel, you look terrible," she laughed and placed a palm on my forehead. "But, no more fever." She brought a cup with a straw to my lips.

"It's water. Drink."

I greedily sucked the water down until I almost choked.

"Whoa, boy!" She pulled the straw away from my lips and sat the cup down.

"Perfect timing to get the flu." She smiled to lighten the blow of her words.

"Is that what's wrong with me? I've never passed out because of the flu before."

"Yeah, well, you've never had the flu during an apocalypse. The flu, a terrible diet, sleep deprivation, and a ridiculous amount of stress - makes for one deadly combination. We've had a few others come down with it, you were the worst, though."

"I didn't know you were a doctor," I said. I didn't know a lot about Melinda. It wasn't like we talked a lot, but she did spend a lot of time with me, before she escaped and brought the Army down on us.

"A nurse," she corrected.

"Even better," I said.

"Always the charmer, Rebel." She smiled and slipped her hand into mine.

"I'm glad you got out, Melinda," I said with honesty. Even if she did come back with the Army. Whatever fate had in store for me, I was glad that this place had been taken down. It had been a long time coming.

"Now, it's your turn," she whispered.

"I'm not going to try and escape," I said when her meaning sunk in. Was she going to help me escape? Was that what she was hinting at?

"They plan on trying all of you, in some kind of court. The leaders will have a representative, along with two reps from the civilians. If you are found guilty, it's a death sentence. They don't really expect anyone to be found not guilty. They were going to hold back your antibiotics, let you die. I can't help you if you stay, Rebel, this is the only way. While she's sleeping…" She jutted her chin indicating something to the left of me. I turned my head and there she was. My captor. She was asleep on the cot next to me. Her features were relaxed, her full lips parted in sleep. She was beautiful, even with her face smeared with a bit of dirt and still wearing her black war gear.

"Well, I guess I have to prove them wrong, show them I'm not guilty," I said with more confidence than I felt, still staring at Hannah. I didn't think that was possible, though. Heather had said it perfectly: culpable. That was me to a tee, culpable. If nothing else, I was responsible for aiding the group and helping them get away with their crimes.

Hannah's eyes twitched in sleep and I turned back to Melinda. She was frowning at me, as if she didn't know what the hell I was talking about.

"Rebel, you don't belong with the rest of these men. I never understood why you were one of them to begin with." She shook her head and fussed with the IV hooked to me.

"Life is funny that way." My eyes were getting heavy. The flu was obviously still causing havoc in my system.

"I threw away your vest," she said. "You don't belong with them."

"They'll kill me," I said tiredly. And they would. I wasn't sad about my cut, but if the brothers saw me without it, I was as good as dead. Technically it didn't belong to me, it belonged to the club. Losing it was a big deal and with my already compromised position, it wouldn't be good. Melinda thought she was helping me, but she might have ushered in my death a bit earlier than we both thought.

"That's not going to happen," she whispered, right before sleep took me again.

THIRTY-THREE

GIVING IT UP FOR THE COFFEE

BABY

I awoke well-rested. I opened my eyes and found myself staring into warm brown ones. He had turned on his side in his small cot. His IV was gone and he laid there looking at me.

I sat up and placed my boots on the ground. If he was conscious, he could have gotten one over on me while I slept. I didn't usually let my guard down like that. I must have been tired. I was supposed to be guarding him.

"Morning," he said in a cracked whisper. His throat obviously still sore from the flu.

I responded with a gruff sound and stood to stretch my legs. I was uncomfortable with the fact that I had slept so hard, but I felt good and rested.

Rebel and Melinda's hushed conversation about escape woke me earlier, and his insistence that he wasn't leaving had reassured me. I had a compliant captive on my hands, but that wasn't a reason to get lax. Anything could have happened, not only Rebel escaping.

"Not a morning person, are you?" he said, his voice stronger.

"I need coffee to be a morning person, and this place is seriously lacking in caffeine."

"I know where it's hidden," he said and smiled around his secret.

"We've searched this place high and low. We've found all of the hidden stores. No coffee."

"Bet you didn't find this one and I know there's coffee, I put it there myself," he said and I frowned at him. *Why was he being so helpful? What was his angle?* Trust didn't come easily for me.

"I'm finding Melinda, if she says it's okay, you're getting me that coffee." I stretched and noticed his eyes trailing up and down my body. *So, that was his angle.* Thought I was hot, or something, and wanted to please me to make me more pliable. I could work with that. I wouldn't do anything to dissuade his attraction. If he thought I was attainable and it would keep him in check, I was more than willing to let him keep believing he had a chance.

I found if you gave guys a bit of hope that they could get in your pants, it kept them on track. You cut them off, gave them no chance, then they got aggressive and hostile. Granted, it was a fine line. If you gave them too much hope, they became pests. Like Duke Nuñez. He was still bothering the crap out of me and all I did was let him do me a few favors. I didn't like to play games, but I would if it made my life easier. I had learned that trick in the military. You were automatically a second-class citizen going in as a female, especially in special-ops. Most of the females were either hard-nosed bitches, or they turned into sluts because they had their choice of men. I liked to ride somewhere in the middle, but as the tours got longer, and the shit got deeper, I found I was slowly turning into a person I didn't recognize. Too hard. Too jaded. It's why I got out of the military and hooked up with MJ Security.

I went to the make-shift latrine and cleaned up. They had set up a hose with clean water for washing and I managed to half-ass brush my teeth. Finger and toothpaste, fantastic.

I found Melinda at Rebel's side after I had searched for ten minutes for her. I tried to hide my aggravation. I really wanted that coffee.

"He's good to go. Where are you putting him?" she asked with Rebel sitting up from the bed, ready to leave the infirmary.

"We'll go get those supplies and then I'll put him back with the other prisoners."

"Is there any way you can keep him separate?" she asked me.

"Where else would I put him, Melinda?" I asked curiously.

"I don't know. He'll be fine, he said he won't try and escape, so maybe with the civilian men." We had brought the civilian men into the main area, out of the elements, and the soldiers and troopers had moved into the offices above. The women had relocated to the gym with the children, some of the men joining them if they were family.

"That's not going to work," I said, shaking my head. "I know you trust him, but I don't. He can't just wander around."

"I'm fine, I'll be fine." Rebel said and he gave Melinda a reassuring smile and stood. Melinda handed him a sweat shirt she had been holding on to and he pulled it over his worn tee.

Melinda didn't look assured but moved out of his way when he walked forward to meet me.

"The stores are kept off base. Did your group round up the men that were on lookout?" he asked.

"We got the ones that were stationed at the floodgates," I responded.

"No, they would have been in houses on Canal, West End and Harrison." We were walking out of the infirmary tent when something hit him hard from the side.

"You fucking traitor!" It was one of the other bikers, his face a mess of cuts and scratches. His hands were zip tied in front of him, but that didn't deter him from landing on top of Rebel and trying to strangle him.

A trooper had been escorting him into the infirmary as we were coming out and he obviously didn't have him under control.

"You were working with them, weren't you? You piece of shit! You've always been trash!" The big man was straddling Rebel and choking him with his tied hands. Rebel managed to get from underneath him and get him into a chokehold, but the guy had to have a buck on him. He was so big and round, Rebel couldn't wrap his legs around him to push him off. They were both swinging at each other like mad men, until Rebel finally landed one that pushed the man back.

I got behind the big man, giving an exasperated look to the trooper who looked startled and unable to move.

"They broke the window and tried to get out. He was bleeding all over the place, I had to bring him to the infirmary!" he defended himself.

When they both fell back in my direction, knocking over a chair and some boxes, I managed to slip my arm over the attacker's neck and put enough pressure on his windpipe to get him to release Rebel, but it turned the biker's attention on me and he began to fight, hard.

He slammed me back and we rolled on the floor. I saw stars as my head hit something. I pulled my knees up and kicked out, getting back on my feet before he could get on top of me. I was quick, but it wasn't necessary. Rebel was at the biker's throat and had him in a hold I had only seen in the Octagon. He had his legs wrapped around the biker's torso and his arm locked around his neck in a weird parody of a reverse hug.

The biker's eyes were bulging out and Rebel didn't look like he was breaking a sweat. This would be the time when a ref would break them up or someone would tap out. The biker lost consciousness and slumped to the floor and Rebel finally released his hold and pushed himself from underneath the big man.

"Nice takedown," I said and held out my hand.

He gripped my palm and used it to get up. "Thanks," he responded.

"I guess we should start treating you like an informant, if you're really going to help us, even if it is only to get coffee. We shouldn't be talking about these things in the open." I looked at the trooper who was staring at the unconscious biker. Probably trying to figure out how he was going to get him into the infirmary now.

"What do the police do with informants?" I asked the trooper.

"We protect them," he shrugged and tried to pull the big man by his arm. All it did was lift his shirt up and expose his gelatinous belly. Gross.

"I don't think you're that good of an informant," I said to Rebel.

"Coffee is only one of my secrets." He smiled and gave me that interested look again. I didn't smile back.

"We'll see."

THIRTY-FOUR

COFFEE AND HOPE

REBEL

"So, you didn't round up any of the lookouts?" I asked once we were out of the infirmary and away from being overheard by anyone.

"No, y'all had men in houses, on lookout? We had no clue," she said, her forehead was crinkled in concentration and I couldn't help noticing how even that tiny movement made her look young and appealing. I tried to force that train of thought away, but it had taken root. She had managed to wash off the dirt from her cheek and it left her flushed and bright eyed. In a different life, in a different time, I would have been panting after her, begging her for a date. But now I would be lucky if she didn't kill me.

"Yeah, there would have been one or two in each house, depending on the time. Do you know how many of the brothers you took down?"

"Nineteen dead, fifteen in custody."

"That leaves six missing," I said without hesitation.

"There were forty of you?"

"Yeah, forty."

"Shit, we got mixed numbers from the civilians and females. No one could give us a specific number."

"We were never all together in a room for anyone to count heads. You'd only know that if you were a brother."

"So these six missing would be the lookouts?"

"It makes sense, three houses, what time did you attack, it was about two in the morning, right?"

"Yeah," I agreed.

"I used to be a lookout. We had a shift change at midnight, but Junior could have changed things up after his father died. He was paranoid. He might have increased the lookout spots or made it two man teams. Anything."

"Or we have three that escaped and three that saw us coming and did nothing."

"I would have run if I was them," I shrugged.

"I would run if I saw us coming too," she laughed, but her eyes didn't reflect her humor. She was obviously disturbed by the thought of a few of us getting away.

"Where's this food store?" She changed the subject. "I'm assuming from this line of questioning that it's not on base?"

"No, we keep food stores in the lookout points that way they would be under constant guard and kept off base in case we were overrun."

"How did they keep the lookouts from pilfering?" she asked.

"They had one brother in charge of inventory, and if he noticed something missing the lookout was the first to be blamed. If it happened we were docked food creds, or reassigned to a new job. It didn't happen often, most of the issues were with the liquor. Senior finally began storing it with the drugs, which was also under constant guard."

"Smart," she said thoughtfully. She looked around the room and not seeing what she wanted began leading me to the office area. "Keep close, don't say anything and look docile." She looked back at me and grimaced.

"I can look docile," I said and shrugged.

"Just 'cause you ditched your leather doesn't make you look less like a biker. Jesus, you're a mess." She looked me up and down and shook her head.

I scratched at my beard. It had gotten a little long. But it was the new trend in apocalypse chic. We were low on hot water and sharp blades in this world. Much easier to let it grow than give yourself a fresh shave each week. It was itchy, but I hadn't given it much thought until she looked at me that way.

"Don't say anything," she hissed. "And walk in front of me. I don't want you at my back." She motioned for me to go up the steps in front of her. We were entering the office area that the soldiers and troopers were using as a makeshift living area.

"Second floor," she said when we got to the first landing and I pushed the door open. We entered what used to be a lobby area. A large table had been placed in the middle and maps of the area were spread out. Radio equipment lined the wall, but they sat dead and untouched, now beginning to collect dust. The room smelled ripe with sweat and mold from the lack of ventilation.

Three men and a woman sat around the table talking animatedly and another man and woman were in a heated discussion in the corner. I recognized the woman in the corner as the female that had been claimed as Senior's property. Her bruises had faded and she was holding herself with confidence, dressed in the same gear as Hannah, battle ready and in control. So unlike the last time I had seen her, broken and only dressed in lingerie. She looked much better this way.

She was talking to an older man dressed in fatigues and he looked exasperated with their conversation. But she looked like she was enjoying herself.

Everyone looked our way when I pushed the door open.

"What is this?" the older guy asked. I recognized his voice from the medical tent.

"Hey Baby!" The brunette walked over to us, looking at me curiously.

"Lex," Hannah said with a little hitch in her voice as if she was forcing herself to stay calm.

I wonder what that's about?

"Found yourself a friend?" she asked holding out her hand to me. "Alexis Winter."

"This is Rebel," Hannah cut off my introduction, responding for me.

"Rebel, huh?" She puffed her bottom lip out and looked at me with a little more apprehension. "I guess you would be the biker, Rebel, the one that was sick."

"That's me," I said trying to look docile and harmless. From the guarded look she gave me, it wasn't working.

"If he's well enough to walk around, why isn't he with the other prisoners?" A tall male stood from the conference table and walked over to us. He was a big guy, fit, for strength, not for show, and his head was shaved, leaving only a bit of fuzz sticking up. It reminded me of the pictures you see of men going into boot camp with their fuzz topped heads and scared looks. This guy didn't look scared, though, he looked scary. He put a protective hand on Alexis's shoulder and looked at me sternly.

"Well, he seems to want to help. What do the police call it? Snitching?" Hannah said with a smirk.

"A snitch is kind of a negative term, don't you think?" I cut in. She glared at me and I remembered I was supposed to be quiet.

"Anyway, Melinda vouched for him. She was actually trying to help him escape, you need to watch her," she said with brows raised to emphasize the deviousness of Melinda.

"Wait, Melinda was worried-" I cut in.

"That's not fair, Baby," Alexis cut in also.

"I hear ya." She held up her hands to both of us. "I like Melinda too, I just think she's too nice." She stared pointedly at me. "I get it, she thinks you're not like the rest of your brothers." She emphasized brothers like it was a bad thing. Which I couldn't really blame her, I didn't like calling them brothers either. At this point there was no love lost. I had never really been one of them, only forced to be by my father. Now there was nothing tying me to them, but circumstance.

"And he was taking care of the children, who also were concerned about his welfare, at least the older ones," Hannah said to the rest of the group. "I think you should hear him out. He could help us. Plus, I'm desperate for coffee." And with that statement, even though she trivialized it with the coffee, a little bit of hope about my possible fate bubbled in my chest.

THIRTY-FIVE

UP AND RUNNING

BABY

The group stared at me like I was from outer space.

Yes, I was defending one of the bikers. Shoot me.

Lex was giving me a weird look. She looked constipated. She grabbed my arm and pulled me away from Rebel with Blake following on her heels.

"What are you asking us?" she said under her breath.

"He told me we're missing six of the bikers and they have food storage stashed at three locations around Lakeview. I'm thinking they have at least one biker at each location. I want to go in and get that food– and coffee. He's going to help. He and Melinda thought I was sleeping, she was about to help him escape, he stayed. He wants to help. That about sums it up." I shrugged, not really knowing if I trusted him, but my gut told me he was legit and I had come to trust my instincts.

"Why would he betray his *brothers* for us?" she asked.

"One of them jumped him on our way out. From what I can tell, there's a lot of animosity there. Something must have happened. We can always ask him."

"I don't trust him," Blake said looking at the biker who stood near the door looking at anything but us.

"My gut says he's an asset." I voiced what I was thinking.

"You're gut says he's hot," Lex laughed.

"You think he's hot?" Blake asked with a scowl on his face. *Great job, Lex.*

"For a biker. He's got that tattooed, bad boy thing kicking. I can see why Baby wants to go on a little adventure with him."

"I don't think he's hot, shit," I said a little loud and my cheeks flamed red when I saw Rebel's head shoot up and look at me.

"What the hell is going on?" Zach walked over and he didn't look pleased. I couldn't blame him; it was like we had reverted back to high school.

"Baby wants to go round up some more bikers with Rebel," Lex said plainly. Which wasn't exactly what I had planned. I was thinking Rebel could tell us where the lookouts were located and we could go out on our own. Bringing him with me was not a good idea. He would only get in the way.

"It makes sense, if you use him to get you close, you can avoid a fire fight," Zach said, and I gaped at him. "If they stayed at the lookout locations, waiting for word, they'll be armed and paranoid. This can work. I think it's a good idea, if you're okay with it, Hannah, I'm for it."

"Really? You'll let her go out there with him?" Lex asked incredulously.

"If the locations are close, we'll be locked and loaded for a quick bail-out. Show us where these lookouts are, Rebel," Zach called out, walking to the table and motioning the biker over.

Rebel leaned over the table and pointed out three locations. They were all relatively close, within ten minutes walking distance, only a few minutes by truck. "I don't think they'll give much of a fight though. If they see you coming they'll give up easily. The brothers that took lookout duty tended to be the ones that didn't use drugs and couldn't take being with the rest of the club for an extended amount of time."

"And what is stored there, for us to take this chance?" Zach asked.

"Only food. They moved everything that was at the grocery into those houses. It was all originally being stored in the temporary trailers, but was moved when Senior started cooking meth."

"What did they do with the medicines?" Blake asked.

"Most of it was used up. The stuff that wasn't good for a high was packed up and kept at the drug store. Anything left will still be there," Rebel answered.

"And did they have any plans for energy, or getting the water back up and running? Any of those kinds of stores?" Poche spoke up.

"No, it wasn't a priority. There was talk of grabbing solar panels from the surrounding houses and hooking them up, but none of them had a clue what they needed. The few men that came back with parts, it was all grid-tied, which was useless."

"And you know something about this?" Poche asked interested.

"The majority of my post-graduate work was focused on sustainable energy. It was the future." Rebel shrugged and we looked at him like he was now the one from outer space.

"Post-graduate work was sustainable energy," I repeated and began to laugh. I couldn't help myself. "And you were living in this shithole with no electricity, running water or communication? What the ever-living-hell?"

"I wasn't exactly someone the leaders consulted with," he admitted. "Plus, they thought I was in law school. If I had told my father I was in architectural design, he would have killed me."

"So, answer this, can you help us wire this place for electricity?" Poche asked, his face eager now, not guarded.

"Yes," Rebel answered simply. "But it might be difficult to get the parts. I know of a place in Mid-City, near downtown, that might have the equipment, but it will be hard to get to. A lot of biters since it's completely surrounded by apartment complexes and condos. I came up from downtown to get here, right after everything went down. It was bad."

"I really didn't expect this," Poche laughed and looked at Rebel. "Who would have thought? Can you lend her for this mission?" Poche asked Blake, motioning to me, like I wasn't standing right here. Obviously the coffee wasn't a priority anymore. Fuck me.

"You want to do this?" Blake at least acknowledged me and brought me into the conversation.

"Sure, why not?" I said nonchalantly, even though I knew this was going to be a shit show. Maybe we could stop at the stores and grab the coffee and I could keep it all for myself.

"Should we send a whole group out?" Blake asked Poche.

"Are we really going to trust this guy?" Lex asked. "I know he's all gung-ho about helping now, but a week ago he was raping and pillaging." She glared at Rebel and he stepped back with his hands raised, playing innocent. I realized she had unclasped her holster.

"I was never into raping and pillaging, personally," he smiled but it was forced.

"Cute," she scoffed.

"If he's willing, we could use the help," Poche clapped Rebel on the back roughly. "What do you think? You're willing to go and round up some converters or what-not for us? How many people you think will be needed to help get the stuff?"

"I think a small team will do it, four at the max. We'll move quicker and we won't need a lot of equipment at first." Rebel offered like he was a tactician or something. "Our aim is to get off-grid inverters and a considerable amount of battery banks. It won't take up a lot of room, but we'll need a truck or van. Are we going to secure the lookouts first?"

"I think this needs to be priority. We can send a team to get the food and secure the lookouts while you head out. I think if we go in armed, any bikers in those locations will come out without a fight. Right now we have enough food, so food isn't a priority. Electricity is our number one priority. We don't have a generator to run our communication stations, which is integral to getting back in contact with chain of command. If you want to help, Rebel, this is your way of helping. Take Murphey and Pratt with you and head out as soon as you're prepped," Poche said quickly and he turned back to the maps on the table. With that, we were dismissed.

"You sure about this?" Zach pulled me to the side and asked.

"Yeah, I've been meaning to check out the city, see how it's holding up," I shrugged.

"Cut the crap, Baby." For once he didn't catch himself on my nickname. I guess it was sticking. "Poche is acting like this is a little jaunt around the city with one of our own people. We haven't been in the inner city since this shit went down and you're being led around by the enemy. I don't know what it's like out there. I don't think this is worth electricity."

"It's not that deep in. I know the place he's talking about, it's right off the interstate. We'll be in and out. I'll have Murphey with me. We've been kicking ass together since before we could drink."

"Which was only a couple of years ago," he retorted and I frowned. He had a point. I thought it was a good argument at least. Murphey and I made a good team.

"We'll be fine, Zach," I said, my tone grave to reassure him.

"I want to go back to our base, we did our job. They have enough men to get things running on their own, I shouldn't be risking one of my own," he sighed and ran a hand over his face.

"It's the right thing to do," I pointed out. "If they can make contact outside of the city, it will benefit all of us."

"You're right," he said. "I just don't like it."

THIRTY-SIX

THE SUPPLICANT

REBEL

Heather Murphey and Hannah Klink were efficient; I had to give them that. They ordered a younger man called Pratt around and packed up a truck for us to use. I tried to be helpful, but it was obvious they didn't trust me and didn't like me wandering around behind their backs. I resigned myself to sit and observe.

They weren't taking much. They packed food, weapons and a few odds and ends- rope, candles, matches, a tarp. Random things that might come in handy. I'm sure they had a reason, I couldn't see it.

"Alright, we're moving out," Hannah said.

"You sure we have enough ammo, Baby?" Pratt asked and I watched in fascination as she grimaced and clenched her fists. I had figured out her nickname was Baby, but she didn't care for it much.

"You planning something I don't know, Pratt? Like an invasion?" she said sarcastically.

"I don't want to be caught unaware," he shot back.

"I'm not humping all this gear if we have to go on foot, which we might, if the interstate is blocked," Heather added.

"It's not going to be blocked," Pratt said.

"I'm not taking that chance. Pack only the essentials. We shouldn't be shooting anyway. Guns should only be used if the situation is desperate. For everything else, blades." Hannah stared down Pratt who was shaking his head as if he didn't agree with her.

She was right. Guns would attract too much attention, it was better to use blades. As if she sensed my thoughts, she turned to me and regarded me. She had pulled a box from the shelving unit the Army was using as weapons and equipment storage. She pulled out my machete. It was the blade I was wearing when they attacked. She had taken it off me and now she handed it back to me.

"Don't make me regret this," she said softly as she placed it in my hand.

"You won't," I said just as quietly.

"I don't feel comfortable only packing handguns," Pratt griped from the corner, an M4 in his hands.

"Shut the hell up, Pratt." Heather pushed a pack toward him, making him put the M4 down. "Here's your gear, get it to the truck. You better wise up quick, kid, and start respecting your superiors." She pushed him out of the room, and followed with her pack on her back.

I strapped my machete onto my waist using the makeshift holster I had fashioned. I picked up the pack meant for me, Hannah did the same.

She began to follow the other two out of the base, but I stopped her with a hand on her shoulder. She turned to me, a questioning look on her face.

"I'm serious about this mission, Hannah, I don't have anything up my sleeve, or any bad intentions. I was a member of the club only because of my father and it was the only thing I knew. I was planning on leaving. I know I'm guilty by association and I accept that. I'll stay and make my amends, and if this is the way I can prove myself, I'll do my damnedest."

"Is that your goal? To prove yourself to my group?" she asked, looking at me with those big blue eyes. She was so tiny, but then she was so unbelievably strong, it was ironic and inspiring. I had always been insecure about barely hitting the six foot mark, especially when I was surrounded by overly aggressive bikers that stood inches taller than me. She was lucky if she was five foot and yet she could probably drop me. It was sobering.

"There's only one person I feel I have to prove myself to," I said honestly. She cocked her head to the side and looked at me strangely and then her eyes widened as she got my meaning. Her lips parted in a quiet little "oh" of surprise.

Her surprise made her features soften as a soft blush crossed her cheeks. I felt myself falling over the edge. I had tried to keep myself in check. I couldn't want this woman, it would only get me in trouble. I would be left wanting, left feeling unworthy. Because I was unworthy. I was nothing compared to her. I was a coward. I was a follower.

And she was everything I wasn't.

I couldn't help but want her. I wanted to be a man she respected, any man would. She was amazing. She was also staring at me as if there could be something there. Something she saw in me. Something that might be worthy.

I could only claim temporary insanity. I was lost in that look. Lost in those blue eyes.

I leaned down and kissed her. Her lips tasted like strawberries from the homemade chapstick I watched her put on ten minutes ago. I had to make it worth it, because I knew it wouldn't last. I knew she would smarten up and see me for what I was. So I put everything behind my kiss.

At first she let me; she might have kissed me back. For one-second her lips parted and she breathed me in. I melted under her soft lips and nearly came undone when with one tug she pulled on my lips with her mouth, opening under my exploration. Then she stiffened as if she suddenly realized what was happening.

I should have seen it coming. I should be grateful she pulled her punch at the last minute. Her fist connected with my cheek. Pulled punch, or not it still hurt like a bitch. I saw stars as I dropped to my knees in front her, a supplicant to her. I had a taste of Hannah Klink. Only one taste. Now, I wanted more.

THIRTY-SEVEN

PROVE IT

BABY

"Don't ever do that again," I hissed, standing over the ballsy son of a bitch. He was on his knees in front of me, he looked dazed. It couldn't be from my punch, I hadn't hit him that hard. It dropped him to his knees, but I think it was more because he didn't expect it.

He probably expected me to be all giggly and ready and willing. He was a pretty man, if you liked that type of thing. If you liked brown bedroom eyes, and full lips that always seemed to be smirking. If you liked strong bodies covered in colorful tattoos of odd things that you wanted to explore. But that wasn't for me. His beard had itched and his lips were too soft. I had hated it.

Liar.

He *was* a good kisser. Or maybe it was because I hadn't been kissed in over a year. I had forgotten what it felt like. I had certainly forgotten what an orgasm felt like. Couldn't even masturbate with the way I had been living. Guys couldn't give a shit about that sort of thing, for themselves. Go in the bathroom and pump one out. Girls couldn't do that. If a girl got caught masturbating– it was like an open invitation to the men around her. I hated double standards.

So, that was why my lips still burned. Why they tingled from the attention. Double standards.

That was the reason I wanted to run my hands through his hair and pull him to his feet and back to my lips. Double standards.

It was only because I was starved for attention.

No other explanation made sense. He was everything I didn't like in a man. He was messy. It was obvious he had some serious shit he was dealing with. Stuff that made him do things that made him a bad guy. *He was a bad buy.* I didn't like messy, bad guys.

He got to his feet and I resisted the urge to help him up. He didn't say anything, only stared at me again with that intense sad look.

Messy or not, I felt that tug in my gut. It really pissed me off.

"I'm not some easy conquest. This isn't a game, Rebel. I hope you understand that if you continue to push I'll have no choice but to push back. And you won't like my way."

"I know this isn't a game, Hannah, and please call me Reid," he said and dropped his eyes. I didn't get him. I saw strength in him, I saw a predator in his eyes. But at times like this, he looked like another victim. I didn't know which was the real Reid. Was he hiding the predator, waiting for his prey to come to him? Or was he truly just another messed up victim of a world gone wrong?

There was no way I could know, unless I let him in. Unless I let him prove himself. And it might turn out that he proved himself to be the wolf, but what if he didn't? What if this wasn't an act? What then?

I didn't even want to think about that. I almost wanted the wolf. That way, I wouldn't have an issue being the hunter.

"I'll make it right," he whispered as if my thoughts were plainly written on my face. "If only so you don't look at me with suspicion anymore." Then he hitched his pack onto his back and walked around me.

I had a feeling this man was going to prove himself in more ways than one. And for the life of me I couldn't figure out if I was excited or scared by this. And why that even mattered.

I was the last to get to the truck. Murphey was in the driver's seat waiting, and Pratt had taken bitch. *Typical.* I looked at Rebel– Reid who was waiting for me by the door and he couldn't meet my eye. It was an annoying habit. I was used to be being stared down.

I got in the back and he followed. *Let the adventure begin.*

It was never ending in this shithole of a life. I thought it was bad when I was deployed. But at least there you had everything provided for you. Need a gun? Requisition one. Need a vehicle to take you somewhere, all you have to do is go get one. Most of the time the meals were hot, unless you were off base, then you had your MREs. Sure, I was being shot at, could be blown up at any moment, but at least there was something bigger to it. Not this constant unknown.

The truck was big, with oversized tires that you needed in the city now. Gaping holes stood out in the street, some had trees growing out of them. Soon this area would be nothing more than dirt roads.

Canal Boulevard, one of the largest streets in Lakeview, named because it was once a canal, was holding up the best and that wasn't saying much. The neutral grounds, the areas called a median everywhere else, were overgrown. The once pretty expanse of grass, peppered with Oleander and Crepe Myrtles were now covered with weeds and fast growing trees were pushing out from the tall grass. I only spotted the spiky leaves of the large Oleander bushes every now and again.

When we got further down Canal, the neutral grounds turned into pools of stagnant water, reflecting the name of the street now more than ever. Before Z hit, the neutral grounds were allowed to settle and sink into the ground because no matter how many times they filled it in, it would collapse. Finally, the city let it settle naturally, put in pretty flowers and dubbed it the "sunken gardens."

It hadn't rained in a while, but before winter hit we had some nasty weather roll through. The water still hadn't drained. With the pumps not working, I wondered if establishing in Lakeview was a good idea. It was filled in swamp, the land forced to comply with human settlers. The water was dying to reclaim the area and without the technology to keep it bay, it was almost inevitable that at some point Lakeview would be sucked back into Lake Pontchartrain and with it Poche's fancy new base.

Another reason to get back to our base, even though we were probably no better. There were no meteorologists to warn us about hurricanes in the Gulf. We wouldn't have a few days to shutter our windows and put the ax in the attic. One day we would look outside and see a black sky, the wind would pick up and the world would get calm. The calm only felt before a bad storm. And we would have a few hours, tops.

Inevitable.

If it wasn't a fucking zombie, it would be a storm. If it wasn't a storm, it would be another biker gang, or some other group of asshats looking to dominate. I pushed away words that bubbled through my brain like black stains, itching to take root.

Why bother?

"Earth to Baby," Murphey's voice cut through my morose thoughts. Pratt was looking at me questionably.

"Yeah, what?" I said sounding annoyed to cover up being out of it.

"Where should we get on the interstate?" Murphey asked.

"Pontchartrain Boulevard, it's a straight shot, you have to cut through the neighborhood. A few blocks up, make a right." I pointed toward a cross street that was coming up.

The houses that lined Canal Boulevard were huge mansions built in the 30s and 40s. It was hard to tell where to turn, so I sat forward in my seat, leaning over the console to direct Murphey. She wasn't a local. I should have been the one driving.

We got to the street, it was just a random side street that looked like all of them, but it was the only one that crossed through and got you onto the back streets of Lakeview. The neighborhood was pretty straightforward, a big rectangle with streets that ran in straight lines. But, since a lot of the main streets used to be canals, only filled in as the neighborhood grew, it was hard to get across them. There were only a few areas you could get through when you were going west or east. It was where there had been bridges and houses hadn't been built.

The side streets were crumbling, badly. The truck rose and fell as if we were on an amusement park ride. Murphey hit a hole hidden in the high grass and the vehicle lurched and slammed roughly to the side.

"Shit," she cursed and revved the engine, forcing the big truck over the rough patch.

"We should have turned on Harrison," Pratt said under his breath.

The truck slammed back down when Murphey managed to get over a hump but we groaned when there was an audible explosion as the tire busted. We hadn't made it ten minutes and our mission was already derailed by a flat tire.

"I know how to change a flat," Pratt declared eagerly and jumped out of the truck.

"Congratulations," I said sarcastically. "Hold on, though, did you even fucking check our surroundings?" I cursed, pulling out my Bowie knife and getting out of the truck with him.

Pratt had gone to the back of the truck and was fiddling with the bed, looking for the spare.

"Of course I checked my surroundings," he scowled at me.

If I was a sadist, this would have been funny. But I wasn't, so I didn't laugh when the zombie shambled up to us and Pratt turned around and screamed like a girl. I rushed past him to take down the single zombie.

He screamed like a fucking girl was a total insult to females everywhere. *Was Poche trying to sabotage this mission by sending this idiot?*

It wasn't a low girl scream either, it was loud and more zombies would be drawn to us from the noise. Sure enough, as I dropped the lone Z, Rebel got out of the truck, followed closely by Murphey. They had drawn their blades as a group of Z rounded the corner and headed directly for us.

There were about ten of them. *Manageable.*

Until the second group came from behind us. And Pratt drew his gun, instead of a blade.

Boom. Boom. Boom. Boom. Four shots. He fired four shots and only took down one Z. Rebel had already dropped three and they lay at his feet while he went after the rest. Murphey was just as productive.

"Put your gun away, you fucking idiot," I yelled and I saw his gun waver. "Put it up! Get out your knife! Now, soldier!" I screamed and he followed orders.

But the damage was done. We tightened up, back to back, hacking at the ever growing horde. As we dropped one, two shambled down the street.

I had forgotten the smell. It had only been a week since my last zombie interaction, but my mind had erased all trace of their wonderful scent. That dead but not quite dead smell. It was a mix of rotting flesh and body odor, mixed with the faint smell of excrement. It was the worst thing I'd ever been exposed to. Give me a dead, rotting, corpse any day.

You get into the mode of killing them. They aren't like killing humans. You don't see emotion, or pain on their faces when you take them out. They continue to stare blankly. Even an animal reacts to pain. These walking corpses keep coming until you take out the head. Then they collapse on the ground, whatever unholy infection that kept the body moving, eradicated.

They shuffled forward, the clothes were tattered on some, others looked fresh as if they had recently turned. There were small ones in this group. The kids were the worst, but easy for me to put down. I didn't have to reach up and stab, or pull a corpse down to my height for a takedown. It was one quick pull, stab and then down it went. I didn't look at its little teddy bear tee. I stepped over it and grabbed for the next one.

Pratt's gun went off again and if I was holding, I would have shot him myself.

How was he still alive in this fucking world?

Douchebags like Pratt were killed off long ago, their stupidity their demise. When Z hit, Darwinism ruled. He must have hid behind the others. Poche probably didn't know how incompetent he was. Pratt had been there in the room, so he had asked him to join us.

I finally came up for air, as the dead fell away from me, taken out by my mad skills. I looked at Pratt, he had two on him. I strode over and yanked one of them off him and stuck my knife right through the eye. I went to grab for the other one, but something dragged me back. I tried to twist around, but there was another one at my feet. It gripped my leg, trying to pull me to its mouth.

Pratt hadn't killed some of them, only injured them so they couldn't stand. How he had done that, I had no clue. But now I was paying for his incompetence. I couldn't break away from the one that had my leg and now there was a nasty zombie arm around me and I could hear the growl of the fucker near my ear. Which was exposed. It was a great place for it to bite me and end my life forever. My body exploded with flight reflexes as adrenaline flooded my system. If I didn't know how to control it, I would have started to panic.

I pushed hard away from it and tried to pull my body from its grip, but it was a strong fucker and I couldn't get leverage because I was trying to avoid the one by my leg. I had thick pants on and boots, but I wasn't taking any chances.

Well, this might be it, Hannah.

I ignored my traitorous mind and gave one big tug. My body flew away from the Zs and I landed hard in the crumbling street.

I scrambled back and looked up, it was Rebel. He had yanked the one off me and it was put down in seconds. He strode over to the one on the concrete and stabbed it neatly through the head. Two more strides and his hand was out and pulling me up. No words, he walked over to Pratt and took out the one that had him.

He was a machine. It was fascinating.

I looked around for more Z to kill. They were continuing to pour into our area. I was completely out of breath.

"We have to make a run for it," Rebel shouted.

He was right. We had to get the hell out of here.

"Left, make a left and run for the 610," I screamed and took off, dragging Pratt behind me. Rebel ran ahead of me. But I didn't see Murphey.

I heard the pounding of boots and looked over my shoulder. She was following behind, gripping her shoulder but running fast. The dead were close behind her.

THIRTY-EIGHT

DOWN GOES PRATT

REBEL

That guy, Pratt, had really screwed us over. I hadn't gone for a jog in over a year, so my lungs were screaming in protest after only two blocks. I raced through an overgrown playground and slowed down enough to look over my shoulder. Hannah was right behind me, followed by Murphey and then Pratt. He looked winded, and Murphey was bleeding from her shoulder.

I didn't want to think about what that meant. A high fence loomed in front of us. It was the sound barrier for the interstate. The nearby entrance ramp led to a series of turns that would take you into the suburb of Metairie or downtown New Orleans and the area we were trying to avoid.

There was no stopping now though. I hung a right and tore through lawns, almost tripping over a bike hidden in the grass. I regained my balance but there were toys strewn all over this lawn and I almost face planted over some kind of plastic slide turned over on its side. *People need to keep their lawn tidy!* The almost trip slowed me enough that Hannah and Murphey caught up.

I glanced behind me again, the dead were close.

Pratt must not have seen me trip, because the clatter of metal and his pain-filled scream clued me in that something bad had happened.

The three of us stopped and turned around. They were on him in seconds. He had gone down and he wasn't getting up. There was no getting up from what was happening. There were at least twenty of them and they all fell to their knees around the fallen soldier. His screams and shouts for help were horrible, but as one we all turned and began to run.

I hated thinking this way, but they weren't following us anymore. We had delivered dinner.

Panting, we entered the interstate. It was wall to wall cars. This part of the interstate was a stretch of cement between grassy fields, not rising until you hit Metairie or merged onto 1-10 to go downtown. If we could make it into the open field that bordered the interstate, we could cross and get to the raised stretch of interstate that headed downtown, which was empty. Everyone had been headed out, not in.

"Come on, I don't want to hang around here," I urged the women. I didn't want to focus on the fact that Murphey had gone white as a sheet, or that blood was soaking through her shirt. I had thought it was her shoulder, but now I saw the angry bite on her neck, right near her jugular. The wound was gushing blood. We needed to get somewhere to treat her, fast. Every time I passed a car, I couldn't help but glance inside. Some were empty. Others held the dead.

"Zombie," Hannah called. She wasn't even out of breath, even though she was holding Heather up and pulling her along.

Hannah's group called the dead, zombies. They went for the straight-forward approach with all things, even the dead. I guess they were zombies. They didn't only eat the brain, though, but everything else was on point. The thing was weaving sporadically, but headed directly for me. One chop of my machete took it out and it fell to the ground.

We crossed over the five lane highway and got to the expanse of empty land in-between the overpass and the flyover bridge.

"Stop," Heather Murphey said in a strained voice. "I can't go on."

"You're going on if I have to drag your ass the entire way, Murph," Hannah spit back and pulled on the woman. "C'mon, we need to get the hell out of here."

THIRTY-NINE

KILL ME, YOU BITCH

BABY

I dragged her for what felt like miles. Miles of uneven ground, high grass, constantly on the lookout for the dead. I didn't even know where I was. I followed Rebel.

The smell alerted me first and I ground to a stop. Heather slipped from my arms like a rag doll.

Rebel, aware of me stopping, came to a halt and bent over panting.

I looked down at Heather. She was still breathing. Her skin was gray, though. Like Martinez. She looked like Martinez had looked. She looked like almost zombie Martinez. Gray skin and she smelled like death. That quick.

She was bit. Her neck was a nasty mess from one of those things. She knew she was as good as dead. I saw it when she opened her eyes and stared at me.

"Kill me." The words might not have had sound. But her mouth worked and formed those words. The blood pumping in my ears was so loud. My heart beat a mile a minute. I couldn't hear her words. But,

I read her lips.

"Kill me, you bitch." I heard them now. "Don't let me turn."

All I could do was stare down at her. There were tears streaking down her cheeks. Rebel stepped forward and I looked up and glared at him.

"Don't even," I hissed and he stepped back, hands raised. I knelt down next to her. I pulled out my knife.

"Murphey," I sobbed.

"Do it," she whispered, her voice a rattle in her throat. "Don't be a pussy." Her eyes closed, she was ready. I did it quick, one slice across her neck and then the next through the base of her brain stem. Hopefully it was painless.

I stood up too fast and lights began popping across my vision. I felt dizzy as if the ground was moving underneath my feet in waves. I crumbled to the ground.

FORTY

BABY

REBEL

She was heavier than she looked. Must be all the gear. She protested when I grabbed her and picked her up. But she was incoherent. I had to find a place to bunker down for the night. We were near some houses; hopefully there was something viable nearby.

When she began to shiver, I readjusted and threw her over my shoulder in a fireman's carry. She must be really out of it. She didn't say a thing.

I exited the interstate and went up the high embankment of the train tracks. When I got to the top, sudden clarity of where I was hit me. We were entering the "Cities of the Dead."

Hannah squirmed on my back.

"Put me down, I'm fine," she complained. I did as she asked and set her down on her feet. She turned and took in our surroundings. The sun was starting to go down. The red sky was bright against the white marble of the raised crypts.

"Great," she sighed. "What the hell happened to me?"

"You fainted," I said honestly.

"I did not faint. I don't faint."

"Whatever you gotta tell yourself," I said a little more bitingly than I usually was. I was worn out. I also didn't want to run through a bunch of crypts with zombies chasing me. I wasn't superstitious, but this was pushing it.

"Ouch." She looked over at me. She was still pale, but color was starting to come back to her cheeks.

"We can bunk in the funeral home. It's probably the safest place in the city. No one would be there," I said.

"Yeah, they're all in the church." She glanced uneasily at the big church that loomed to the east of us. She shivered and swayed on her feet again. I grabbed for her with the intention of helping her but she pushed my hand away. I couldn't believe she was standing at all. I wouldn't be able to function if I had gone through what she did. I went to her again, not caring that she didn't want my assistance, this time she let me wrap an arm around her but she got a glare in.

"I got this, let's go." She pulled away from me and marched down the tracks and into the cemetery. She stumbled once, but righted herself and kept marching forward. Leaving me and my chivalry behind.

Row after row of crypts were in front of us. Each tomb was like a little house. Some even had iron fences around them. Grass and weeds poked out from the "streets" between the tombs, but it was in relatively good shape. This was one of the newer cemeteries, catering to the Lakeview and Mid-City people. The tombs showed fairly recent dates, and their facades were still glossy and glittering in the sunlight.

I trudged along with Hannah at my side until we reached the end of the row. The path of tombs led to a circular drive and a squat but expansive building that was built to resemble a house. Not one car was parked in the lot. It would be empty.

I went for the door and was relieved to find it locked. If it was still locked, there was no one in there. I used my machete to force open the door and we stepped cautiously into the building, the stale smell of decay the only indicator of safety. There was no smell of rot or body odor.

I pulled out my flashlight and shone it into the building. I had been to one funeral here, so I knew they had three or four viewing rooms, and two break rooms. I led Hannah to the left and we passed a viewing room with the coffin still in place, dead flowers surrounded the box. I hoped to God there was nothing in there.

Around the corner was a break room and to my great pleasure, a water cooler. I grabbed a tiny paper cup and filled it with water, pushing it into her hands. She gulped it back greedily and then stuck it under the dispenser for more.

We drank our fill and then I found some towels and began to clean off. She followed suit, not saying a word. I peeled off the thick layers of clothes, starting with the heavy leather jacket I had been given in place of my cut from the club. It was warm in here. I wouldn't need it.

When I was done cleaning up, I pulled cushions off the sofas that lined the hallways and brought them to the break room and piled them on the floor. Then I shut the doors and propped a chair up against the handle just in case.

Hannah paced back and forth, digging in the cabinets, looking under tables.

"I have these." I pulled MREs from my pack.

She nodded and came over and sat next to me. I filled one heating element with water and activated it. I placed the two meals in the cardboard packaging it came in, with the heater in the middle and sat back and waited. In those twelve minutes it took for the MRE to cook, she sat there quietly next to me. She must have used some kind of lotion or soap because she smelled like lavender again. She sat next to me so close I could feel the heat of her body against my right side.

I poured some of the drink mix in a bottle I had in my pack and shook it up. The mixes were full of vitamins and sugar. She needed to get something in her system. She was physically fit, but we had lost two of our team, had run over five miles and we were now on our own, in the middle of a cemetery and half of our supplies were in a truck miles away.

She took the bottle from me and gratefully chugged it, then took the MRE packet I handed her and began to slowly chew the contents.

I followed her lead, chewing the bland tasting meal. I didn't know what I was eating. It tasted like sauce, whatever it was. The MREs came with a little bottle of hot sauce, but I couldn't find it. I must have dropped it when I pulled out the pack.

We finished our meals at about the same time and I grabbed hers from her hand, got up and put them to the side for trash. When I sat back down, I didn't intentionally sit closer. I was close enough to touch her, though. Our legs were stretched out in front of us, separated by only inches. I had never been this aware of someone's hand, the placement of their thigh or the shift of their head since I was a teen bracing for my first kiss.

The whole right side of my body tingled with awareness and all we did was sit there, not talking, staring at the one point of light coming from a small lantern in this dark room.

"Thank you." She broke the silence with a pained whisper. I don't know what she was thanking me for. It might have been for the MRE or the water, or for setting up the cushions. Maybe it was because I was respecting her need for solitude. I would probably never know, so I nodded my head as if I were wise and knew what she was talking about.

Then the toughest woman I had ever known just sort of collapsed next to me. She fell into my side, her head on my shoulder, and her body shook as silent tears ripped through her. I wrapped her in my arms and pulled her closer. She was so small, but she fit to my side perfectly. I held her tight and let her cry. I didn't say a thing. I didn't say meaningless platitudes like, "It'll get better," or "she's in a better place," because personally I didn't believe either of those statements.

This world was not going to get better. There would be no happily ever afters in a world where people ate each other. Where men like me took advantage of the weak. And how could there be a God in a mess like this? How could an all-knowing God authorize something like this? If there was no God, there was no heaven, so after we closed our eyes forever, it would be blackness, or worse, reincarnation.

I couldn't imagine being a child in this world. Might as well strap a sign on your back that says, "dinner."

I was lost in my black thoughts when her shaking stopped and her breath evened out. She had fallen asleep. In my arms. I guess instead of being all glum, I should have paid attention to the woman that made my body tingle. The woman I had been obsessing over since she pointed a gun in my face. *Baby.* The nickname fit.

FORTY-ONE

IN TROUBLE

REBEL

I awoke with my back stiff and my shoulder asleep. There was something warm and soft pressed against me. I was still propped up against the wall and Baby was draped over me. When I moved to get life into my arm, she moaned in protest and moved in closer, her arm draping over my lap.

It was morning and as a typical male in his early twenties, I awoke showing off my virility. She moved again slightly, coming to and trying to figure out where she was. She looked up at me, her big blue eyes blinking away the sleep. I was so grateful I had left the lantern burning, I got to witness this moment, instead of it being lost in the darkness.

"Morning," I said to her.

"Morning." There went that blush again, that flare of red came to her cheeks so easily. It flamed hot when she realized where her hand was resting and what it had stimulated. She moved it quickly, but didn't break eye contact.

I almost pulled her back when she pushed away from me and got to her knees. I almost took advantage of her grief and her confusion. *Almost.*

I let her go, and she went to the door and moved the chair. The light washed over us. It must be late in the morning judging by the amount of light in the outside hallway.

She glanced at me, a halo of light around her as she stood in the doorway.

"I'm going to find a bathroom," she said and all I could do was nod. I was in trouble.

FORTY-TWO

GIVING IN

BABY

The place was alight in the morning sun. I hadn't seen a day this pretty in a while. New Orleans winters were generally gloomy, foggy and overcast. The humidity never left no matter how cold it got. It was the kind of cold that got into your bones and never left.

But not this morning. The sun shone brightly, the sky was a bright blue with only a few clouds to mar it. Birds flew in and out of the trees, celebrating the morning and the feel of spring creeping into the city. It was beautiful, but all I could do was stare morosely out of the glass front of the building. The day did not reflect my mood.

Murphey and I were the kind of friends that wouldn't see each other for months and then start up the conversation right where we left off. When I left the Army, we hadn't seen each other much. She had come to New Orleans on leave one time, but that was about it. Even though she had been stationed close, she was still living the military life and didn't agree with me becoming a mercenary.

It didn't matter though, she still would visit and we would pick up right where we left off. That's why she came looking for me after Z hit. She knew I was alive. She knew I would help her. And now I had let her die. I had always been stronger in hand-to-hand, Murphey had preferred the air, going SOAR, the Special Operations Aviation Regiment, after Airborne, while I went Ranger. I shouldn't have let her handle that on her own. I should have been there for her.

A little movie projector in my head replayed the events, reassuring me there was nothing I could have done. We were outnumbered, and I was in the shit myself.

There was nothing I could have done.

My thoughts repeated on a loop. The knife went into her neck again and I shivered.

I needed a bathroom. I wandered around the place until I found a bathroom. I stripped and cleaned up using the water in the toilet to do a bit of wipe down. I used water from my canteen to brush my teeth though, I had my priorities. Sink was for bathroom, toilet for cleaning. The world was fucked up.

I got dressed again. The day might be bright, but it was still chilly. I went to find Rebel. I had been confused when I woke up. I had woken wrapped around him. To make it worse, I had enjoyed it. I felt safe. He took care of me last night. Honestly, he had taken care of me this entire trip. I didn't know what to think about that. I never had someone take care of me. *Never.* Not even my parents, when they had been around. *It was weird, it was off, it was warm.*

I found him standing in the hallway using the mirror in the hall and the light through the windows to shave. He was shaving his beard off using an old fashioned straight razor. The kind that folded and was used by barber shops.

I felt my entire perspective shift. I stood there staring at him like a fool, my gut twisted in knots.

"I found this in the director's office. It was in a fancy leather case." He held up the case and smiled. With half a beard and a big smile on his face he was ridiculous and attractive. My stomach flipped. My perspective shifted two more degrees.

Why not?

Really, why not? I had worried about what Rebel would prove to me on this mission. I shouldn't have, because the only thing he proved was that I could trust him. That he was a good guy.

He looked back to the mirror when I didn't say anything and continued to hack away at his beard. He was not used to using a razor of this kind, it was apparent by how he was doing it. I walked up to him and took the razor from his hand.

He looked down at me and I pushed his chin up.

"Why are you shaving your beard, Rebel?"

"Because, you don't like my beard, Baby." It was the first time I didn't cringe at my nickname.

I grabbed the lotion he had been using and smeared it onto his cheeks and neck. We stared at each other the whole time. I could see the confusion in his eyes. I'm sure mine gave nothing away, since I was as confused by my actions as he was. I knew that while doing this I wasn't thinking about Murphey and that knife.

The knife and her neck.

I placed the blade against his neck and he swallowed nervously. My mind flashed to Murphey's neck again. And what I had done. How I had killed her.

"I'm not going to hurt you," I whispered, not know if I said it for him or me. I began to shave his face. Long strokes, and I paid careful attention around his nose and chin. By the time I was done, his cheeks shone and his face was smooth.

I touched his chin and then ran my hands over his cheeks and face. I inspected my work, I had done a good job. He was almost pretty without his beard.

He pulled the razor out of my hand and flipped it close, he put it in the case and set it to the side. Then he encased me with his arms, he placed both of them on either side of me and pressed me against the table. He leaned in close, but he didn't say a word. He didn't have to. We were both thinking it.

I wanted to forget.

He took my mouth and kissed me with a passion I had never experienced before. I felt the warmth of his attention travel from my lips through my chest and nestle between my legs. It was an amazing feeling and I wanted more. I wanted to forget. I wanted to lose myself in this man.

I opened my mouth for him and his tongue licked at the insides of my mouth. He gripped my hips and pulled me closer. My arms involuntarily went around his neck. My whole body was pressed against him. His erection was hard and insistent on my stomach.

His hands went to my ass and he pulled me even closer to him, I could tell he wanted more. My head fell back as he picked me up and placed me on the small hall table. His cock pressed between my legs as I wrapped my legs around his waist.

"Damn," I moaned as his lips found my neck and kissed down the sensitive vein and then bit my ear. His hand left my ass and went to my stomach, pulling my tank top out of my pants and lifting it up to expose my sports bra.

He fumbled with the tight material until I had pity on him and pushed away for a second to pull it over my head. I kept these babies strapped in tight, so exposing them felt different and heavy. He stared at me, his eyes dilated, his mouth open. I knew I had a nice rack, but I didn't expect to stun him.

"This is where you say something like, 'nice tits' or-" He bent down and captured a nipple in his mouth and I moaned in response.

"Nice tits would be a lie, these are the most beautiful pair I have ever laid eyes on," he said around licks.

"Yeah, that's much better." I moaned again as he did something with his fingertips and his tongue. *That rocked my world.*

I wasn't exactly educated in the bedroom. I had sex a few times, but it never felt like this. It was rushed and sweaty. Rebel had shit happening to places on my body I didn't even know could feel.

I wanted him all over me, I wanted him inside me. Whatever he was doing I wanted him to do it to me over and over again. I wanted to forget. I wanted to give in. I wanted to feel him.

I told him so.

FORTY-THREE

THANKS FOR EVERYTHING

REBEL

I was drowning in her. In the smell of her. In the taste of her. She was amazing. She was so responsive. With each kiss, I fell deeper into her. All I knew was her and everything from now on would be her. It scared me and excited me and made me want to run as far and as fast as I could into her arms.

She made me forget the world outside. There was nothing but Hannah. Her skin was so smooth. How did she get her skin so smooth? She should have been disgusting, sweaty and a little bit rank in this world without showers and toilet paper. Instead she smelled of lavender, her skin felt like velvet and her hair like silk.

She was turning me into a poet.

I wanted to take it to the next level. I wanted to strip down, bare her to the world and recreate every last fantasy I've had since puberty. She slid her hands under the hem of my shirt and her soft fingertips trailed over my chest. She yanked at the material, then pulled the shirt over my head. Those same delicate hands kept busy as they moved to my waist, pulled at my pants and popped the button of my fly open. She pulled the material aside and my whole body froze in anticipation.

She murmured her wants. They were the same as mine.

"I need you, Rebel," she moaned as I dropped down in front of her and tugged on her pants, pulling them lower, over her knees, exposing flesh and that warm apex where her legs met that I wanted to touch so badly. I pulled her forward on the table, sucking on her bare thigh, licking and tasting the wonderful flavor of her skin.

"Fuck," she screamed as I couldn't wait anymore and I pushed forward, licking down and across her labia. I spread them with my fingers, pushing her open as far as I could in this awkward position, with her pants still stuck at her ankles because we had forgotten her boots.

I couldn't get a good angle to pleasure her, so I stood and slipped my fingers across that tight nerve bundle at the top of her pussy. She reacted immediately, pushing forward against my hand and crying out my name again and again. I slipped a finger inside of her and pushed it in and out. My dick throbbed against my jeans jealous of a finger.

I needed to get her somewhere better than this hallway. Somewhere I could spread her out and lick her from top to bottom. Taste her as she came all over my face.

I stepped back, my reserve was at an all-time low. I was about to spin her around and take her right here, pants around her ankles, ass in the air. But she didn't deserve that. She deserved to be treated like the hero she was. I didn't want to screw her in a funeral home in the hallway because we wanted to forget that we had lost two people.

Stop.

I pushed back and away from her. The look of confusion in her eyes, the hurt and the rejection, almost stopped me right there. I didn't want to see that. I almost went back to her. But I couldn't. I couldn't do this to her.

I heard a noise and my head jerked in reaction. They stood at the window leering at us, their jaws hanging open in abject hunger. Their fists beat feebly at the window, their legs almost bent forward from the pressure of the ones behind them.

"I didn't even hear them," she said as she jumped off the hallway table and pulled her pants up. She buckled her belt and then grabbed her bra and shirt off the floor, putting them on quickly. I did the same and looked at the biters congregating in the front of our building. They would draw more.

This could have been bad.

"I guess that's our cue," I said resigned and she looked at me, now fully dressed again. She walked over and patted my now bare cheek. She got on her tip toes and kissed me lightly on the lips.

"Thank you," she said and I didn't know if it was to signify that things were now over between us, like this was a one-time thing that would never happen again, or if it was a random 'thanks for the almost orgasm.'

Again, I nodded and took it. I guess I would find out later. *If there was a later.*

FORTY-FOUR

ITCHY

BABY

My skin was flushed and I was itchy, not with an actual irritation, but something underneath that made me want to run a few laps and do a hundred push-ups. I wanted to grab Rebel and throw him on the floor and ride him like the slut I had deep inside of me. It was a fairly rational thought, considering I was still burning everywhere he had touched me. It played in contrast to the other thoughts screaming in my mind for attention. The ones that made me want to collapse to the floor and sob like the baby I was. Give up and let the world take me. It was a hell of a combination of reactions. I was an emotional wreck, something I was not used to.

I needed to be back in control.

I didn't think I would ever be able to feel like this. Five parts grief, three parts anger and two parts horny. *Okay, maybe four parts horny.* I was a mess. I had regarded Alexis, Blake and Zach as possessing something I couldn't understand. They must have different priorities than me, a different perspective that allowed them to be so distracted in a world like this, to engage in such sexual behaviors while mourning loved ones. It was something I couldn't understand. *Until now.*

I had joked about it, I had mocked it, but I had never understood it. There was so much darkness, how could anyone let sex take priority? How could anyone look for love in a world like this?

Yet, with that tiny touch of sexual awareness Rebel had awakened in me, I understood. With that brush with bliss, I craved it more than anything I had ever craved before. I wanted it. I wanted more. If I couldn't have it in a world like this, I might as well give up. I might as well sit down, let Murphey's death break me and let the world eat me.

I didn't want the world to break me. I wanted to break the world. And I wanted to do it with Rebel.

I looked at the zombies pressed against the glass. One day that might be me. It might be sooner, rather than later. Why did I have to sit and focus on that and only that? Why couldn't I feel bliss?

I needed to find him. I wanted to run him down and rip his clothes off and say, "Let's do this shit." He had gone somewhere. He was disturbed by the peeping zombies. I could see that all over his face. He felt like he was putting me in danger. Again, that weird feeling of being taken care of. It was a hard thing to get used to.

I found him in the director's office, a distracted look on his face.

"Hey," I said quietly so I wouldn't startle him. He knew I was there, though. He looked up and smiled, holding up keys.

"A hearse, it'll be in the back. Hopefully gassed up."

"I hope they don't have someone in there," I laughed and walked to him.

"Doubt it," he said and followed me as I tugged on his hand.

"So, where do we go? Back to base and abandon this mission? Or press on?" I asked.

"Press on. I'm not going back to that base with two dead and nothing to show for it." I frowned as his words hit.

"You're afraid of what will happen?"

"No, I don't want Pratt and Heather to have died for nothing," he said and I could have kissed him. I wanted to. But something in his tone and face had me holding back. It wasn't the right moment.

"They won't. We'll get the equipment and get Lakeview back up and running."

"Works for me," he said as he casually rubbed my back as if he had been touching me like this for years, instead of a few hours. His touch again ignited a fire underneath my skin and my thoughts dipped back between my legs.

There would be plenty time for that. We had things to do.

FORTY-FIVE

GO SOLAR

REBEL

The hearse was gassed up and ready for us, no coffin in the back. There were two of them in a hidden garage behind the funeral home. We chose the black one. We only had two packs between us, so it wasn't like we were hauling a lot of gear. This would work.

The solar energy warehouse was only a few miles from our location. We could get on the interstate and be there in five minutes if there were no obstacles.

The hearse started up with only a little resistance. I let it run for a few minutes to get the engine used to running again.

It was a newer model, so it shouldn't give us any trouble. I let it run as Baby opened the garage doors manually. There was nothing waiting for us, so I took my time as I rounded the corner, not wanting to run over anything and derail us again.

When I passed the front, the biters at the window turned and began to follow us, but we were on wheels and they were on foot. There was no contest. I pulled onto Canal Boulevard, and made a right, heading toward downtown.

We reached our first obstacle at the overpass at Metairie Road. The area underneath the pass was flooded. It was submerged under what looked like four feet of water. This was a common thing in the area and the reason for the big pumping systems at the foot of Pontchartrain Boulevard. Those pumps ran on electricity, though and with any heavy rain these low areas flooded.

Some genius of a city official put in a measuring stick on the columns at the lowest part so commuters could know how much water was in the pit. They would know it was four feet deep and they wouldn't take a chance and try to drive through it. That was how I knew I wasn't going to make it through.

There was an easy way to solve this. I went up the down ramp on this side. It's not like I would be driving into oncoming traffic and it would also place me on the same side as the solar energy warehouse.

There were more cars on this side, since this headed out of the city. They were stopped randomly and thick, but I drove on the shoulder of the road until it opened up and I could get a good speed and head into the city. The cemeteries faded to houses and then to warehouses. The warehouses led to the jail and my mind focused on the possible state of that building. Was the jail full of zombie inmates? The ones locked in cells, did they turn, or just slowly die of dehydration, forgotten?

I shuddered at the thought and Baby looked over at me curiously.

"You think they evacuated the jail?" She looked at the brand new complex that sat close to the interstate. The large wall that surrounded the imposing building was spiced up with the city's team logos painted over the cement facade by inmates.

"Probably not, they didn't during Katrina, not until after. I heard a bunch of them drowned in the lower floors, it was bad."

"That's sick." I shuddered again and she grabbed my hand. It was such an innocent gesture but it meant so much. Again, that flicker of hope.

I thought about my brothers being held at the base. I hadn't given them much thought, but thinking about those inmates drowning in their cells brought them to mind. Poche had mentioned they would be tried, I would be tried, but what did that mean? Was it to be a court like before? Would there be a jury? And what happened if they were found guilty? Would they be put in a jail for life, or something else?

I was thinking of it separate from myself, but chances were I would be tried the same way. It was only fair. I was a Southern Clansmen, by birth, by right and by association. I had never embraced that lifestyle, but I had imitated it. I had faked it for my father. For his approval and his acceptance. Which, even with all the faking, had never been achieved. When the Army found me, I was boldly showing my association by wearing their patches. I had the tattoos on my body, not yet covered up, not yet eradicated. Even though I had planned on doing it, *one day*. The story of my life.

"What will they do to the brothers that are found guilty?" I asked, changing the subject, but she followed along as if her thoughts followed my same rhythm.

"Firing squad," she said simply.

"That's, that's…" I had nothing to respond with.

"It's the only way. What else could we do? We don't have a jail, and we can't rehabilitate. If the truly guilty of your brothers were to be exiled, released into the wild, so to speak, they would only go out there and do it again. We would be allowing them to take other women, rape and kill indiscriminately. This, in my opinion, is letting them off easy."

She looked at me regretfully, but didn't release my hand.

"That's putting a lot of responsibility on the men with the guns. Taking a life, many lives as they stand there. It's not right."

"We've done it before," she said quietly.

"Who? And what did they do?" My voice was rougher than I expected.

"The men that sold Alexis to your group. We found them and that was how we handled the situation. They didn't have a court though. Your men will at least have a court. If any of them are innocent, at least they'll have a fighting chance."

"The situation," I said and looked over at her. "Do I have a fighting chance?" I asked.

"I don't know. Doing this might give you a pardon. Hell, it should. I'll make sure of it. You're not a part of that group."

"I was though, Baby. I was one of them. I might not have done what they did, but I sure let it happen. I saw your friend, Lex. I was there when she was brought in. I was there when Senior claimed her. I did nothing, I'm just as guilty."

"I don't want to talk about this," she said, her voice panicked.

"It's only the truth," I said lightly, catching sight of the large banner that advertised the solar power company. It was brightly colored with a picture of a woman smiling brightly and tearing up her energy check. It was still crisp and bright, a beacon that stood out from the rest of the dreary city.

I pulled to the side of the road. We were mere feet from the building. The interstate was so close to the warehouses that were built before the modern conveniences of cars and the burden of traffic jams. We could jump to the balcony that surrounded the upper floor of the building with ease.

"What kept you there?" she asked and turned to face me.

"Fear," I said honestly and I saw her eyes become shuttered in unmistakable disgust. It was only right. It was what I deserved.

"Fear of what, Reid?"

"Fear of being out here, on my own. Fear of them tracking me down and beating the heck out of me again."

"They did that?" she asked.

"Regularly," I laughed. "It's why I began taking MMA, I was done with being beat down. It didn't help though, once I beat them one on one, Junior began to get his buddies to wail on me all at once."

"Why stay?"

"It was all I knew." I looked at my hands, suddenly ashamed.

"Well, now you can know something different," she said earnestly. She squeezed my hand and smiled. It was the first time her smile was reflected in her eyes. She was beautiful. I wanted to pull her in my arms and tell her everything would be okay. That we would go back and we would be fine. That I was the man she needed. That I could make everything right.

I didn't, though. Because it was a lie. I smiled back. We got out of the hearse. I left the keys on the dash. We stayed on alert, but it was a ghost town. Baby crawled up on the ledge of the interstate and jumped.

My breath caught in my throat, but she made it with ease and looked at me as if to say, "your turn."

I got onto the side rail and made the mistake of looking down. I was at least thirty feet up and a few of the dead wandered under me, their moans unheard but their movements gave them away.

If I fell, I would be like a snack falling from the sky for them.

"Jump," she urged me. I did. I coiled up all my energy and pushed off from the side rail. It was nothing, only a few feet, but it was the scariest thing I had ever experienced.

"That was insane," I said after I had calmed down and got a look at our surroundings.

"That was easy," she laughed.

"Sure, you do that all the time."

"I used to, but out of airplanes. You've never lived until you've jumped from a C130 to a Blackhawk."

"Okay, you win, I'm a pussy."

"I think that's the first naughty word I've heard you say. Figures it would be in reference to a part of the female anatomy."

"I curse," I frowned, knowing it was a stretch. I had gotten out of the habit when I realized how crass it made the other brothers look. I cursed with them, always playing a part.

"No, you don't. I think it's sweet." She got on her tiptoes and kissed me lightly on the lips.

I deepened the kiss and she moaned against my lips. It took every bit of strength in my body to pull away from her. We didn't know what was in store for us in this building.

"Let's get this over with," I said. "I really have something else I want to do."

"You and me both," she said and smacked me on the ass.

FORTY-SIX

WASH ME

BABY

We were on a balcony with a glass, hip high wall that enclosed a large area. A trendy outdoor table set sat in the corner and a high-tech looking panel was embedded into the wall near a sliding glass door.

The balcony was set lower than the interstate so you weren't staring right into traffic, but all you got was a view of the cement of the raised road. It wasn't exactly a room with a view.

Rebel went to the sliding glass door and pulled on it. It opened. I guess no one expected someone to jump from the interstate to get in. We banged on the wall to attract the attention of any dead in the building, but nothing moved, nothing moaned back at us. All clear.

We walked into what was a surprisingly posh, efficiency apartment. I looked around in disbelief. It was clean and the air was fresh. It was like a dream. Like we had stepped back in time to a PreZ moment. I slid the door closed behind me and looked around the room in fascination.

"The HVAC is working," he said and went to a panel on the wall, clicked a switch and the lights came on.

"I thought this was a solar company, not an apartment complex?"

Rebel held up a pamphlet from the coffee table.

"It's a showpiece." He flipped through the pamphlet. "They were trying to showcase the future of energy independent living in an apartment setting. Everything in this apartment is hooked up to self-sustainable energy. It should all work." He looked around. There wasn't much to the place. It was little more than four-hundred square feet, only a low wall and a few steps separated the bedroom from the living area.

He went to the sink in the kitchen and turned the tap. Water ran from the spout. It ran clear.

"This is fantastic. I would have been trying to get hired on with this place if I saw this."

"Can we stay here indefinitely?" I asked, sitting down hard on the white sofa. I got up quickly when I realized I was dirty and this sofa was bright white. Rebel started to open up the cabinets. There weren't many, but they were pristine. They were also empty.

"Not much food," he laughed. He opened the last cabinet and revealed a washer and dryer combo. It was one of those tiny ones that could only do a small load.

"Now, that is gold!" I dumped my pack on the floor and pulled out my extra clothes. I kept a shirt and a pair of pants rolled up in the bottom. I had hand-washed them in our homemade detergent, but all my clothes smelled perpetually like campfire.

I squeezed past Rebel and shoved them into the washer machine.

"I can't wait to put on a shirt that smells like fabric softener!" I yanked my armor vest off and threw it on the ground, then yanked my shirt over my head, putting it in the machine to join the other clothes. I really wanted to wash my underwear. It was rather trivial, but I really missed crisp, clean underwear.

As I pulled my boots off, Rebel made an odd noise in his throat and I stopped to look up at him.

I was about to strip down to nothing in front of him. Which really shouldn't be a big deal since his face was buried between my legs a few hours earlier. Nothing he hadn't seen already. But we were in that awkward, 'are we going to do it again and maybe this time complete it' phase. He must be of the impression that what we did earlier was it.

I wasn't. In fact, I had every intention of him finishing what he had started and now I would have clean underwear to put on after. *The little things.*

"It can fit your clothes too," I said innocently. "You should probably," I smiled coyly, "Strip."

He pulled off his shirt and handed it to me. I put it in the washing machine. We both undid our heavy boots, putting them to the side. I undid the button of my pants and pulled them off. Being efficient, I brought the panties down with the pants. I didn't meet his eyes, I turned around and shoved them in the washer, then ripped off my sports bra and put it in with the rest.

I turned around to find him completely nude also, his pants held in his hands, covering up a part of his body I was most interested in seeing. I hadn't realized the extent of his tattoos. They were sexy as hell. I had always had a thing for ink, but it had to be just right. His right arm was covered from wrist to shoulder in an intricate mix of bright colors and swirling Escher-like patterns. The designs crossed his shoulder and plummeted down his chest and across his stomach. His chest was mostly done in blacks, with only a little bit of color peeking through every now and again. One of those spots was the confederate flag and the words of his MC, but it was obvious he was trying to distract from that with the rest of the design, including an intricate clockwork bird design that overtook all of it, mixed with interesting flowers and *was that a sugar skull?* I would have to inspect his tats a little more.

I held my hand out for his clothes and he handed them to me. He was erect. His cock was hard and protruded proudly from his body. I hadn't been with many men, but he was impressive compared to the others. He was thick and the length was enough to give me pause. I might be taking on a little more than I could handle.

His cock jumped and I looked up and met his eyes guiltily. I was staring. I turned quickly and put his clothes in the wash, sprinkled some detergent on the top and turned the dials until I thought it was the right setting.

With a slam, I closed the door to the washer and turned around to face him.

"Now what do we do?" I asked.

FORTY-SEVEN

SPIN CYCLE

REBEL

I grabbed for her. I pulled her to me and didn't think about what I was doing. My hands were all over her naked body and my mouth was exploring everything it touched. I led her backwards, our lips colliding, our breaths mingling. She even stepped on my toes a few times, but I couldn't care less.

I broke away to get my bearings and then swept her up in my arms and threw her on the raised queen size bed. I took a few moments before I joined her to stare at her beauty. She was breathtaking. Her skin was absolutely flawless, the perfect pale shade of peach, with not a mole or freckle to mar the tone of it. She had designs down her side, they looked like words mixed with flowering hibiscus and leaves from her armpit to her fit stomach.

"What does this say?" I moved onto the bed with her. The words were in a different language, maybe German, and they flowed over her skin in an inspiring work of art. It was a great piece.

"Whoever fights monsters should see to it that in the process he does not become a monster. And if you gaze long enough into an abyss, the abyss will gaze back into you," she quoted from memory.

"Nietzsche, kind of deep for a grunt," I laughed. She looked at me with fake offense, which was hard to do since we were both naked and quoting a long dead philosopher.

"The fact that you even know who that is blows your bad-boy biker persona out the window," she teased and rolled her eyes.

"I thought I blew that one out the window a long time ago," I said and moved over her, capturing her mouth so she couldn't respond. She kissed me back with an eagerness that had me dying to spread her legs and claim her, but I held back. I kissed her face, her chin, her neck until I had my face buried in her beautiful tits.

Another perfect part of her body. I kept finding new ones.

I sucked a nipple into my mouth and she moaned, pressing up against me. I ran my fingers through the wet folds of her pussy. She was soaked and I slipped two fingers into her easily, smiling around her nipple as she bucked and cried out.

I sucked on her nipple as I penetrated her with my fingers. In and out, quicker and quicker, I moved them inside of her. I wanted to be buried in her, dick deep, but I wanted to make her come more. I ran my thumb over her clit in a circular pattern and fingered her until she spread her arms and thrust her hips up against my hand, screaming my name as she orgasmed.

"Rebel," she called.

"Call me Reid." I requested and I stopped touching her.

"Please don't stop," she moaned.

"Then what are you going to call me?"

"Reid, fuck me, dammit." She grabbed me by the neck and pulled me down for a kiss. I used my knee to spread her legs wider to accommodate me.

We both gasped as my dick nestled between her legs and barely penetrated her. She was so wet, she was dripping.

I pushed in, entering her slowly. She was tight, but wet so it was a contrast in feelings. I used my arms to prop myself up and concentrated on the act of sliding deeper into her.

Our gazes locked as I fully seated myself inside her, making sure she could take all of me without pain. She showed no sign of discomfort, only pleasure. Her cheeks were flushed and her eyes were glazed, her mouth open slightly as she panted from the sensation.

I held still, focused on our joined bodies and the warmth that spread over me.

She was the first to get anxious and began to push up against me. I pulled back, withdrawing almost all the way out of her and then pushed back into her hard.

This time she screamed my real name without any prompting. Might as well reward her. I stimulated her clit, rubbing it with my thumb as I pumped my cock into her tight pussy.

She came undone around me. I felt the pulse of her pussy as it gripped my dick and the pleasure overtook her. I gave her a moment to enjoy the wave of sensation, then I slipped my arms under her thighs and pushed her legs up so I could get even deeper inside of her.

I slid my hands down her legs and gripped her by her ankles as I began to pump hard into her. I set a rough pace, but I was lost in her, lost in the feeling and she was urging me on with her wonderful little noises of enjoyment. When I felt another orgasm overtake her, I was done. It hit me hard and fast and suddenly I was jerking into her, my orgasm a hot flash of sensation that broke me open and left me dizzy and murmuring words that made no sense.

I pulled out of her and she whimpered at the loss, but I was spent, my eyes grainy, my body heavy. I didn't want to crush her. I moved to the side of her and pulled her to me, reaching spastically for the covers to pull over us. I had never felt this content in my life. I might have said it out loud. But I didn't care. I wanted her to know what she did to me.

FORTY-EIGHT

SHATTERED

BABY

I was sore, especially between my legs. I awoke and I could feel the pulse of awareness there, from the amazing sex I just had. I wiggled and felt him hard against my back. He was either awake too, or he had serious morning wood. We hadn't been out that long. I didn't feel like we had slept much. Enough to refresh.

His arms snaked around me and cupped my breast, squeezing tightly.

Awake then.

He pinched my nipple hard and I cried out from the pain, pleasure of it. Not able to resist I arched my back and pushed against him. His hands went to my hips and pulled them tight against him, his hard cock pressed into my ass. He slipped it between my legs, not entering me, only stimulating me. My legs were still closed and as he pulled himself in and out of the juncture between my legs it created a unique sensation.

When he found my clit, I shattered. The feeling was amazing and I couldn't control my body. I wanted to move in five different directions at once. I wanted to kiss him, I wanted to fuck him, I wanted to take him with every part of me, but I was facing the wrong way.

"Inside of me, Reid," I moaned. I needed him.

"Not yet, Baby," he cooed. His pace picked up as he circled my clit with those amazing fingers. He sucked my ear lobe into his mouth and held me tight to him as he pumped between my legs but he never entered me. He took me over the edge with his clever fingers.

I came with a shout and a lot of jerking against him as my body flooded with a pulsing sensation.

"That's what I needed," he said as he rolled me to my back and kissed me generously on the mouth.

"Ditto," I managed to get out between breaths.

"C'mon, get up, I'm sure if the washing machine works, the hot water heater works. I can't even remember what a hot shower feels like."

"Not something I want to hear from the guy I just sexed up," I laughed but he looked like he regretted what he said. "Oh, speaking of that, I gotta put the clothes in the dryer." I got up from the bed quickly.

"I already did that, not too long ago. You were sleeping, I didn't want to wake you."

I could have kissed him. Or declared my undying love for him, which was a little overboard for him doing laundry. But it was thoughtful and people didn't do thoughtful things for me. Especially now that everyone was focused on surviving.

Instead of opening my mouth and making a fool of myself, though, I dragged him to the shower.

The shower was probably the biggest thing in the tiny apartment. There wasn't a bath tub, only an enclosed shower with two shower heads and a shallow bench along the back wall for holding soaps and shampoo. There were no toiletries in the bathroom, so I fished out the homemade stuff I had begun to really enjoy from my pack.

I had helped Grace make the soaps once and it was enough for me, but I enjoyed watching the process. She had this strange combination of watered down ashes and animal fat that she would "cook" and then combine at different times. For scents, she would boil in certain herbs she collected. I preferred the lavender bars. It grows like a weed at our compound so it's plentiful.

Rebel was already in the shower and he opened the door to let me in, taking the soap from my hand and sniffing it.

"I love this smell," he smiled and began to lather me with the soap.

"So do I," I said, sighing as he meticulously cleaned me from bottom to top. He might have paid special attention to a few areas, but I wasn't complaining.

When he was done, I took the soap and returned the favor. I also paid special attention to some parts which wonderfully came to attention in my hand. Before long, I had him moaning and thrusting his hips against my hand as I slowly stroked him. I watched his face as I brought him fully erect in my palm.

The floor was cold, but I didn't mind as I got to my knees in front of him. I licked out and tasted the head of his dick and the salty pre-come that leaked from the end. He grabbed for my head and held me tight as I sucked him into my mouth.

"Damn," he cursed as I began to suck harder along his length. I swirled my tongue around the tip as I pulled back and began to stroke him with my hand and lick the head.

I took him deep again and again. He lost his balance, and had to brace himself on the back of the shower as I aggressively took him deeper into my throat.

He held on tight to my head and pumped into my mouth. I let him control the pace, I took it and let him fuck my mouth.

Suddenly he went stiff and I thought he might come, I was ready, but he pulled out quickly. He yanked me to my feet and spun me around. His hands pushed me up onto the tiny ledge of the shower. With one quick motion he entered me, quick and hard. He pressed me hard against the back wall of the shower and plunged into me repeatedly.

Holy. Shit.

I held on for dear life as he took me with a vigor I have never experienced before during sex. Never before had I felt this way. I was a mess of conflicted emotions and sensations by the time my orgasm overtook me. I scratched his back with my fingernails, unaware of what I was doing as he roared my name and emptied inside of me.

He broke me into pieces. I didn't think there was anything that could put me back together again–except maybe more Rebel.

FORTY-NINE

YOU AND ME

REBEL

Somehow we ended up on the floor of the shower. She sat curled in my lap. We were caught in an endless kiss that I didn't want to break, but the shower was sputtering. We had used up all the water in the reserves.

I grabbed a towel from the rack outside the shower door, and wrapped it around her. I dried her off as she stared up at me with those big blue eyes. She was soft looking right now, so content. I couldn't rectify this Hannah with the tough soldier, but they were one in the same. And I wouldn't have it any other way. While I enjoyed this pliable and sexual side of her, the soldier was who I had first been fascinated with. The one whose smile never met her eyes.

As if on cue, she smiled at me, her eyes soft, her skin flushed from the hot water. I wanted to pull her to me, put her in my pocket, and hide her away. I wanted this moment to last forever. I wanted to get down on my knees and beg her to stay with me in this tiny apartment. We could scavenge for food half the time, the other half we could spend in bed.

But I didn't say that. We had responsibilities. Or she did, at least. I was along for the ride. I had been along for the ride since I laid eyes on her.

With a sickening feeling I pulled the clothes from the dryer and handed them to her. I grabbed my own and began to dress in the warm clothes. It couldn't have lasted for forever. I knew this, but I couldn't help but feel a little apprehensive about leaving this place.

"The batteries should be downstairs somewhere. They probably have them stored in an inventory area. I'm hoping they also have a truck available that we can load up. Once we get those in place, we can drive out of here."

"Drive out of here," she repeated my words.

"We have to go back. We have to let them know you're okay, and--"

"And Murphey and Pratt aren't." She gritted her teeth and took a deep breath.

"I would stay here with you. I would try my damnedest to make it work– to survive, you and me." I took her face in my hands and looked down at her. Her eyes had gone hard, but they softened with my words.

"Just you and me," she whispered as she kissed me gently.

I pressed her against the countertop, my fingers trailing lightly down her side. The smell of freshly washed clothes in my nose, a smell I hadn't experienced in a long time. I felt her fingers at my waistband. Her cold fingers brushed across my bare stomach and with a willpower that would make superman jealous, I broke away from the kiss and rearranged my dick so it wouldn't be so obvious what I really wanted to do.

"As much as I want to, as much as I want to march you back to that bed, bend you over and – *damn*." I ran my hand over my face and got back on track. "We have to go back."

"I know," she said, but looked away as she said it. "It's just that once we go back, I'm, well, I'm the grunt and you're the…"

"Biker," I finished for her.

FIFTY

REALLY GOOD SEX JUST ISN'T ENOUGH

Baby

The search for the solar shit was rather anti-climactic. With the bullshit we went through to get here, I almost expected to have some near death experience in the halls of this solar company's plant, but it was eerily deserted.

We slammed the hilts of our blades into the walls of the metal building to attract attention, in case there were any dedicated worker zombies hanging about. Nothing. It was quiet. We wandered up and down the building hallways until we found the storage area. Everything was neat and in place. We even found the service trucks parked in aisles near the back bay of the warehouse. Some were even loaded, as if waiting to go on a job. We chose an empty one and tried to start it up, but the engine didn't even sputter. It had been sitting there too long. They were odd looking trucks and a few had cords coming from them.

"They're electric," I said as Rebel tried to start the next one to no avail. The big start button should have clued us in, but our minds were else-where.

"The warehouse should be run on solar, like the apartment. I don't know why they aren't holding their charges." He followed the cords to a bank of batteries and bent over them. "Oh, they're not plugged into an inverter. It looks like they charged up the batteries, drained them and then switched them out." He unplugged one of the cables and plugged it into another set of batteries.

"Check the last one, it should have a light to indicate it's charging," he said.

I walked to the last vehicle in the line and sure enough, there was an indicator that it was charging.

"Yeah, like a cell phone," I laughed. I missed my smartphone.

"Will probably take about six hours to charge, that's plenty of time to find the parts."

"But not to get out of here before dark," I pointed out.

"I guess we'll have to spend the night here," he smirked.

"Shame," I responded with a grin.

We decided it was a good idea to take two of the vehicles and the battery banks that were used to charge them. We couldn't siphon gas forever. These vehicles would be an asset. We should return and take all of them, but right now we would take as much as we could.

We filled each truck with batteries and a few panels, but not much. We didn't want to take up precious room in these small vehicles. Most of the panels we would be able to get from off the houses in Lakeview. This was all about the batteries and the inverters which were meant for off-grid set-ups.

When the last battery was placed in the back of the truck, I closed the door and looked at Rebel who was fiddling with the batter bank.

"It's charged. This must be some powerful stuff." It had only been three hours. We still had two hours of daylight.

I looked toward the stairs and then at him regretfully. He shrugged.

"I think we should get back. We've already been gone too long."

"What's one more night?" I said but I knew it wasn't right.

"We'll have more nights, just not here," he said but I didn't believe him. He looked away, anywhere but at me. He knew it too. He was lying. When we got back, everything would be different.

I wanted to grab him, shake him, punch him, something to get him to fight for this. Was he giving up so easily? *Was he ready to go back and just roll over?* His usual MO?

He had forced me to believe in him, to accept him. And now he was ready to wash his hands of everything. His life. His freedom.

"We can stay! We don't have to go back. we can take one of these trucks and get the fuck out of this city. We don't have to stay here. We can go anywhere. Make our own life," I argued.

"No, we can't." His voice was stern.

"What the fuck is wrong with you? Why are you so scared to go out on your own? We can do this!" I hit him in the chest and he grabbed my hand.

"And what? You give up everything you and your people have put together? For what? Me? A guy you just met? You don't even know my last name, Hannah. I sure as hell don't know yours. You'd do that? And for what? Because we had good sex?"

His words cut like a knife, which was what he intended. I wasn't dumb. He was scared. He didn't think he could make it on his own, even if he did have someone like me at his side. It was the reason he had hidden behind the gang, even before Z hit. Whatever, I didn't know his last name, but I had him pegged. Reid, Rebel, whatever the hell he wanted to go by, was scared. He was scared of letting people down. He was scared he wasn't good enough. And at this moment in time, he was right.

"My last name is Klink, by the way, which I did tell you. And yeah, it was really good sex, not good enough for you to stop being a fucking martyr though. C'mon, asshole, let's get you back so you can pay for your sins." I didn't stop and wait for him. I unplugged the first truck and loaded up the battery bank into the passenger seat. I saw he was done with his so I went to the garage doors and got them open.

Two Zs wandering in the street turned our way and began shuffling in our direction. I let Rebel pull out and then I got in my truck, pulling it forward and through the doors. The Zs were close, but I had enough time to get out and close the doors behind me. Then I got behind the wheel and flattened the two of them as I tore after Rebel.

FIFTY-ONE

HOME SWEET HOME

REBEL

My thoughts plagued me the entire way back to the base. I was always in my head way too much and the shit I told Hannah messed me up. I didn't need her throwing her life away for me. She had already lost so much. I shouldn't be the reason she isolated herself from the rest of her friends.

My mind flashed to the other day, back in Lakeview. Hannah with her friends. I had watched her with Alexis. I had watched as she interacted with the two big guys that ran their base, Zach and Blake. They were more than just her friends. That group was a tight unit, like family. I couldn't pull her away from that for my selfish wants. Because of the bad decisions I had made. I had to face my sins, as she had called them.

The trucks were quiet. They called no attention to us as we weaved down the crumbling streets of the fading city. I maneuvered through the back streets until I made it onto Canal Street. Once a bustling area of commerce and tourism, the street was a mess of detritus and the large houses stood dark and brooding behind their overgrown lawns.

I passed a red street car that used to be a common sight on this street. The old tracks had been refurbished and reinstalled so the people of

New Orleans had more public transportation. What was once thought to be outdated was cherished and brought back after Katrina, and now it was forgotten again. The red paint, so vibrant only a year ago, was now faded, the windows broken, splatters of what might be blood peppered the sides.

It was tragic and yet fitting.

Canal Street led us back to the "Cities of the Dead" and the end of the street car line, where Lakeview began. I pulled around the curve, keeping an eye on Hannah's progress behind me. So far, so good.

We were about to turn on Canal Boulevard, only a few miles from the base when I remembered at the last minute that this way was blocked, it had to be. If the interstate drop was underwater, the dip under the train tracks on Canal Boulevard would be under water too. I motioned out the window for Hannah to follow me into City Park. It was the long way around, but a less populated area so it might work out better.

I pulled onto the quiet road that ran parallel to City Park. It was once one of the largest urban parks in North America, now it was on its way to being a forest. The great oaks that lined the street had been a pleasure for me, before the end of the world. Now, they looked ominous. Their reaching branches hid the dead and other menaces behind their thick trunks.

The park was overgrown, small trees jockeyed for sunlight, on the way to turning this stretch of land back into what it once was before people. The vegetation had overtaken the road in some spots, forcing me to drive onto the shoulder. As we passed the main area of the park and the large stadium that hugged the interstate and cut through the park, the number of dead roaming aimlessly along the side of the road increased.

The theory was they liked to go west. Most packs we've run into were heading west. They would be stopped here. The Orlean Avenue Canal ran from Lake Pontchartrain to the train tracks that cut through Lakeview. It was a large drainage canal surrounded by high levee protection walls. With the spillway gates now closed, there was only one way to go west, go around. It seemed to be too much for the dead, they wandered aimlessly in circles, confused. They would speed up as we passed, and start to follow us, but would trip in the high grass and weeds and get sucked into the boggy ground.

The ponds and smaller canals that lined the park were all over-flowing, turning this area into a swampy mess. It had once been a well-maintained stable which led into a golf course, now it was returning to the old ways. Marshland.

At the last spillway gate, I slowed and let Hannah pull to the side of me. There were two stern looking soldiers where there had once been two of my brothers. Hannah got out of her vehicle with her hands in front of her.

"Hannah Klink. We left with Murphey and Pratt a few days ago. You can verify us with Poche if you need to," she said as calm as I had ever seen her. Their guns were pointed at her, frowns on their faces.

"I recognize you, you're with Miller and James's group, come on through. Where's Murphey?" the solder asked at the last minute and Hannah's features tightened. She shook her head and the soldiers dropped theirs to look at their boots. Nothing more needed to be said.

The one closest to us wrapped his hand around a rope tied to one of the plastic blocks and pulled it to the side. Hannah returned to her truck and the soldiers waved us through.

We rolled up to the base moments later. A tall brunette was waiting for us in the back parking lot. She had her hands gripped together nervously, but her face lit up when she saw the vehicles. It was Alexis. I sat in the driver's seat as Alexis yanked Hannah out of the truck and pulled her into a hug.

I felt like such a voyeur, but I couldn't look away. I watched as Hannah tentatively wrapped her arms around her friend and then the telltale shaking of her shoulders started. It must have surprised Alexis because she looked down with surprise at her friend, but she held on tight.

"How did they die?" I was startled by Poche at my window. He leaned in and took a look at the stacks of equipment behind me. "They radioed in from the gate. I tell ya, I didn't expect this shit. Murphey was one of my best."

I got out from behind the wheel and looked one more time at Hannah. She was being led away by Alexis. She never glanced back.

So this was what it felt like to be debriefed. It was tiring. I told the story of Murphey and Pratt's deaths three different times. Once to Poche, then again to Zach and Blake and then again to Tammi Ryan. Luckily they didn't want to know details about the rest of the adventure, but they did want to see what I had gotten and how we could hook it up. They had even poached a few panels while we were gone.

It was a fairly simple set-up and I showed them how to do a basic unit that would run a small appliance, realizing too late that I should have hoarded my knowledge - if I was the only one that knew how to do this, they might keep me around longer.

I hooked up the inverter that would feed the communications area and my head shot up when I heard the distinct sound of gunshots. At least five shots in quick succession. I looked around me for some kind of reaction from the people in the room. Nothing. I was being watched by one of the troopers who made it clear he was only here because he was ordered to be.

"Are we shooting at the dead now?" I asked.

"They ain't shooting the dead, firing squad, *buddy*," he drawled.

They were shooting my brothers. The ones they found guilty. Hannah had warned me.

"That's the second one today. I watched the first trial this morning. Brutal. Went quick, the good ones are going to be tomorrow and the next day. Gonna put the girl on trial, the one that they are bringing from the island. Heard she went crazy and tried to kill Alexis, you know the tall brunette that has the Marines panting after her?" He looked at me, waiting for a response, so I nodded.

"Then they gonna put up your leader, Junior. If you ask me, a bullet is too good for that one." Again he waited for a response, but my mouth had gone dry.

"Wonder when your trial is scheduled for?" He laughed and crossed his arms, jutting his chin out and staring me down.

I wonder.

FIFTY-TWO

FIRING SQUAD

BABY

"Where are the boys?" I asked Alexis. We had pulled up chairs in the alcove of the main building. She had taken out a bottle of vodka she had claimed for herself. She poured a shot and pushed it in my direction as gunshots rang out in the distance.

"They're in the trial."

"We're already doing it?" I asked. I grabbed the shot glass and knocked it back. It burned something awful, but the burn quickly faded to a nice warmth that spread over my whole body. I had left him out there. *I hadn't even looked back. Making him pay for his stubbornness.*

"Yeah, we started today, we're doing two or three a day. The first one was found guilty. I'm guessing from the sound of that gunfire, the second one was guilty too."

"Who'd they choose to be judges?"

"Blake, Zach, Poche, Ryan, Grace and a civilian that was with the troopers, called Phoebe. Romeo is filling in if Blake or Zach can't do a trial, and Poche and Ryan have back-ups too."

My whole body tensed up and Lex noticed it. I grabbed the bottle and poured two more shots, throwing mine back quickly so she would stop staring at me. I had been able to hold my liquor before Z, but there wasn't much liquor left so I was becoming a lightweight. My head buzzed pleasantly.

"What are you freaking out about, you look nervous? I haven't seen you this shaken up – ever. Did something happen with Murphey you're not telling me?" She looked at me curiously and sipped her shot. *Who sips shots?*

"So, they're putting all the bikers on trial?" She raised her eyebrows when I didn't answer her question.

"Yeah, all of them, Clara and two of the civilian men are also up to be judged." *All of them.* She made a face, thinking I had reacted because she brought up Clara. Clara Clark, Blake's ex-wife. Clara, the woman who tried to kill Alexis in some weird, misguided attempt to win Blake back. Clara, the reason Lex had been sold to the bikers and landed us in this mess. Lex shouldn't have to even say that woman's name.

"They're not going to kill her, are they? I don't see them doing that, fucking bleeding hearts. And I'm assuming Blake won't be a judge on that one?" I asked, channeling anger over the ex, instead of the other emotions that wanted to take root. Anger was easier to deal with, I could work with anger.

Alexis shook her head and explained, " Zach won't either, Romeo is stepping in for the two of them. Putting it at a five person panel, so no ties. That will give her three hard-asses and two civilians. There is no one else that can judge her without bias, even Romeo is pushing it. He's voiced that he doesn't feel like he should. But they keep ignoring him."

"Are you going to be there?"

"I have to be, I have to speak for her."

"What do you mean?" I asked.

"The idea is that witnesses will speak for the accused, that's how they're deciding guilt or innocence. Whether you speak positively or negatively will sway their decision."

"And if they're guilty they-" I was hesitant to say it.

"Firing squad. Or that's been the sentence so far. But it's all been some bad shit. Zach told me about this morning's trial, some guy named Eagle. Fucking sociopath. This gang was full of them."

"Crap." I poured another shot.

"Yeah," she agreed and grabbed the bottle from me.

I stumbled when I got up from the table, but only a little bit. I had done a few too many shots with Lex. I had needed some kind of escape. But the alcohol was making my emotions more pronounced. *Maybe I shouldn't have done quite so many.* But, I wasn't scheduled for any kind of watch or mission, which was a first. No reason to stay sober.

I came to a stop as I walked toward the temporary bunks where I would be sleeping. A large chalkboard had been affixed to the wall and dates and names were scribbled on it. At first I thought it might be a watch schedule, but names stood out. Jazz, Eagle, Tiny- those weren't soldiers.

Lex came up next to me and looked at the sign with me.

"The trial schedule," she said what I had already figured out.

I focused in on one date, four days from now. And a name, scrawled haphazardly.

Rebel.

FIFTY-THREE
NO BETTER

REBEL

"We did give it careful thought, Rebel. Your work here has been nothing but helpful and we found four of your brothers along with a considerable amount of food stores because of your tips. Don't get me wrong, we'll advocate for you on those points. We have to make sure this is fair and it's been decided that all the members of the Southern Clan will be tried. We've also taken testimony from the civilians and we're bringing charges against two of the civilian men because of crimes they've been accused of during the Southern Clan's occupation, so we're doing this as fairly as we can," Poche told me as he led me to my new living area. It was an empty office on the second floor. Still basically a cell, but not as heavily guarded as the third floor.

"It's the only way we can bring justice back to this world," he said as he closed the door on my new quarters, leaving me alone.

He was right. It was only fair that I would stand trial with the rest of my brothers. If I was judged and found guilty, then that was that. Poche was the only one from the military that showed me any respect, the other soldiers and troopers had no respect for what I did to help. In the day that I had been back, I had taught three of them how to hook up a system, charge the batteries and hook up a battery bank to an appliance.

Now they were done with me. I had no more information to give. No more usefulness. I wasn't allowed out of this room from now until my trial.

I would wait until they decided if I was guilty enough to kill.

I hadn't seen Hannah once and I didn't expect to see her again. She shouldn't waste her time with me. I overheard one of the soldiers joking that she and Alexis were getting drunk downstairs. She probably regretted what we did. I basically took advantage of her. She was looking for a shoulder to cry on and gave her a lot more.

I was no better than the rest of my brothers.

FIFTY-FOUR

MY BUSINESS

BABY

"What's the matter?" Alexis's words weren't slurred and she did more shots than me. It helped that she had practically a foot and thirty pounds on me.

I was still staring at his name. I guess they had decided to give him a trial. She had said *all of them*. I hadn't wanted to believe her.

She followed my eyes to the board and turned to me with a questioning look on her face that said, "spill." *I wasn't talking.* I looked away and she stepped in front of me.

"Lex, really, I love you, but get the fuck out of my way." I went to walk past her, but of course, the stubborn broad stepped to the side, blocking me again.

"One, you told me you loved me. Right there, I know something is screwing with your head, and two, you need to spill, now." She was an obstinate one. I would have to come up with something to get her off my back.

"Look, I think he did a good job, he helped us out. He helped me out.

He saved my life. I don't want to see him taken out by a firing squad. He was with that group because of his father and because he was too scared to leave and go out on his own, it shouldn't be a death sentence."

"And that's all?" she asked, ever the insightful wench. I guess I couldn't blame her; I gave her the third degree when she was going back and forth with the boys.

"Yeah," I shrugged.

"I call bullshit," she chirped with a smile.

"You can call bullshit all you want, that's it. That's my story, I'm sticking to it."

"What's bullshit?" One of the boys in question came behind Alexis and put his head on her shoulder. Lex was a tall girl, but Zach had her by a head. I used to have some major hots for Zach when I first started with MJ Security. It couldn't be avoided. He was a walking, talking piece of male perfection. But those feelings had faded quick when he proved more of a leader than a possible love interest. Not to mention he had no interest in me whatsoever. He actually hadn't shown any interest in a woman until Lex came along. And now, well, he sort of shared her with Blake. It was a weird arrangement that I didn't get, but they seemed to make it work. It got a lot of whispers, but they didn't let it bother them.

They didn't care. They did what made them happy.

"The fact that Baby is lying about something, something that I think has to do with Rebel," Alexis answered.

"I'm not lying," I said stubbornly.

"Well, you sure as hell aren't sharing all of it." She crossed her arms and stared me down.

"If you know something, Hannah, we need to know about it. Did he tell you something when you were out there?" Zach, of course, was missing the direction of this conversation.

"Yeah, *Hannah*, what did he *tell* you when you were out there," Lex snickered and Zach caught on from her tone.

"You hooked up with the biker?" he said, truly surprised.

I threw my hands up in exasperation.

"Jesus, you did." Lex's voice was surprised. She really didn't think I had, she was only harassing me.

"That's rather out of character," Zach said diplomatically.

"He's a good person," I hissed, looking around me to make sure no one else was all up in my business. I hated people in my business, judging me and my actions. I would put up with Lex, or even Zach, but no one else. No one needed to know my business. Well, maybe Rebel.

Lex looked at the chalkboard and then back at me and whispered, "I'm so sorry."

FIFTY-FIVE

GUILTY

BABY

Lex asked me to go to Clara's trial with her and I agreed. It was the only one I planned to go to, I didn't want to witness the show. It was a shit show to say the least. They were holding the trials in the empty area that was once the drug store. Anyone was welcome to attend, as long as they didn't have a job to do.

The place was sparsely attended for this trial, no one but our group really knew about Clara. A few of the women, former Clan property, were seated in the audience, which surprised me. Blake was already seated in the front and Lex went to him. She sat next to him and slipped her hand in his, I sat on the other side of her. Zach was at the back of the room, trying to be unobtrusive, but I knew this was eating him up inside. I was there when he told Blake he wanted to be the one to kill Clara. From his expression that statement still held true.

The room hushed as the judges came into the room. Poche, Tammi Ryan, Romeo, Grace and the civilian I didn't know. They came out and sat behind temporary tables and looked out on the crowd.

Poche cleared his throat and stood. "Bring in Clara Clark Miller," he announced.

Two soldiers led her in. She looked terrible. Her once bottle blonde hair was halfway grown out, her dark roots down to her ears, the ends faded and washed out looking. There were dark circles under her eyes and she had lost weight.

They sat her in a chair off to the side so she could look at both the judges and the audience. It was a good position, she could see the people that spoke for her and the ones that would judge her.

"Clara Clark Miller, you are here today accused of attempted murder and disregard for the safety of your compound. Your reckless actions have caused terrible repercussions and you are here now to be judged. Once a verdict is given your sentence will immediately be carried out, do you understand this?" Clara nodded warily and looked into the crowd with a pleading look in her eyes. Her gaze landed on Blake and tears began to stream down her cheeks.

She looked pathetic, *but Clara was a good actress.*

"We ask if anyone in the audience will speak for Clara, do so now. The floor is open." Poche sat down and looked directly at Lex.

Lex stood and glared at the woman who had wronged her.

"I speak for you, Clara, I want you to know what you've done to me. How you tried with everything in your arsenal to take away the man that I love. I'm here to tell everyone how you lied and maneuvered your way into our compound and then did nothing to benefit our group. How you realized you couldn't get your way with me around so you decided to take me out of the picture. How your stupidly constructed plan almost got both of us killed, hell, it almost endangered the entire compound," Lex took a deep breath and continued.

"You attacked me, held a gun to my head and made me smash through the gates of our safe haven, not giving any thought for the people behind those walls that you endangered. You were ready to kill me and dump my body; you didn't plan for me to fight back."

"You're lying!" Clara called out. "You were trying to get rid of me! You held a gun to my head! The only reason I'm sitting here and you're over there is because you've got Blake all wrapped up in some weird sex– "

"Enough!" Poche interjected and Clara shut up fast.

Alexis faced the judges.

"She had me run through the gates of the compound until we got to a deserted area. I had a knife, so I stabbed her in the leg. When the gun went off, I crashed the SUV. The sound of the crash or the gunshot, I won't ever know, brought men to our location. They were looking for victims and we were a gift. They took both of us and sold us to the Southern Clan. If it weren't for Clara, I would have never ended up here, at this place. I was beaten regularly...and other things," she said, her voice wavering. "But I got out."

"Yeah, I helped you get out," Clara shot out.

"Bitch, I'm the only reason you're alive and sitting in that chair. I got your ass out. After everything you did to me, I saved you," Alexis hissed and Clara kept quiet for once. "I'm done." Lex threw up her hands and sat down. But then thought better of it and stood back up.

"Wait, maybe a little more. Clara is a spoiled, user of a human being. She's used to getting her way. When she doesn't, she strikes out. She'll do and say anything to get what she wants. I can't stand her, but I don't think her actions are deserving of death. I don't want her anywhere near me, but dead is dead. And frankly, taking her life is not worth scarring the soldier who has to shoot her."

Lex sat back down and did a one finger tap off her forehead in Clara's direction who was staring at her in open contempt. She held two fingers out to indicate this was the second time she's saved Clara's life. I've got to give it to Lex, she had a way with cutting right to the chase.

"Is there anyone else that will speak for Clara?" Poche asked the crowd.

"I will." A woman from the back stood. She was too skinny and her hair hung in limp locks down her back. There was once beauty there, but a broken look had taken root. What was once a pretty girl was now hidden by dark circles under her eyes and sallow skin.

"I can't say anything about what Clara did before she came here. I can't even say that Clara is a nice person. She kept to herself. I do know she was regularly chosen by Spider. So was I. I wouldn't wish Spider on my enemy. He's the worst of the worst. If you can think of something depraved or sadistic, Spider liked it. I told myself when I heard about Clara that I would at least stand up and tell you this. She has paid for her crimes, like I have paid for mine." She sat down abruptly and the room fell deathly quiet.

"Anyone else?" Poche asked after a moment. No one volunteered. The only thing that broke the silence was the sound of boots on linoleum. I turned in my seat and saw Zach leaving the room.

"Thank you for your testimony. We'll adjourn and have a verdict soon." Poche and the rest of the judges walked out to decide Clara's guilt or innocence.

We waited for what felt like hours in tense silence. The only thing that marred the quiet was the sound of Clara's subdued sobbing. I was there to support Lex, but all I could think about was Rebel. Who would speak for him? Would there be girls that stood up and spoke of depravity and sadism? That would kill me. That would kill him, what was I talking about?

I heard the creak of a door and the judges filed in. Romeo looked grimmer than ever, if that was possible. Grace was crying. Ryan and Poche were stoic and they remained standing as they looked at Clara. The accused.

"Clara Clark Miller, you've been accused of attempted murder and endangering your compound. We find you guilty."

The wail that came from her mouth was ear splitting and I tried not to feel for her, but it was impossible. She was a heinous bitch, but I would be evil myself if I took glee in this.

"Your crimes have earned you exile. You'll receive one knife, one change of clothes and three days' worth of food. You are not allowed in Lakeview, or anywhere near the compound in New Orleans East. If you are spotted near these locations, you will face the penalty of death. Your sentence will be enacted immediately. Graf, please get her a walking pack and escort her to the 17th Street canal bridge."

Clara sobbed. *Exile.* This changed everything.

FIFTY-SIX

HOURS TO DAYS

REBEL

The hours bled into each other, hours to minutes, minutes to hours, hours to maybe days. Everything spun and twisted together. No one came to visit me, no one came to talk. The only interaction I had was when I was taken to the bathroom twice a day and when I was brought my meals. I didn't even know how long it had been. One day, two days? A week? I hadn't been paying attention. I laid on my cot and stared at the ceiling.

I shouldn't have come back. I should have stayed in that tiny apartment. With her.

Deep down I thought my actions would get me some kind of special consideration. I had told them where some of the men were hiding, which would most likely result in their death. I had killed my brothers, men I had grown up around, to prove myself to a group that had deemed themselves righteous. For a girl that hadn't looked back.

Someone knocked on the door. I ignored it. *It's not like I had a choice.*

FIFTY-SEVEN

EMPTY PROMISES

BABY

Alexis was a pain in my ass. She wouldn't leave me alone. She wouldn't let me go and hide. She also wouldn't let me anywhere near the vodka.

"We drank it all," she said as I glared at her.

"You're lying," I scoffed.

"If anyone deserves vodka, it's me," she said in her haughty annoying voice.

"You did get your boyfriend's ex exiled, yeah, you deserve it." I stumbled over the alliteration and she scrunched her nose. "You should be celebrating. Go get the vodka. Let's celebrate."

"When did you become a lush?"

"Regret is a bitch," I sighed.

"That's deep," she scoffed and threw herself on the cot next to mine.

"Don't you have something to do? Aren't you supposed to be one of the leaders or something?" I said annoyed at her interruption of my pity party.

"My mad leadership skills aren't really recognized by this bunch of misogynists. I'm okay with that, they have too many meetings. That's why I'm here. Zach and Blake are up there meeting with Poche and Tammi again. I just want to go home," she sighed.

"You and me both," I yawned.

"So, there's a reason I'm here." She sat up on the cot and looked at me.

"Oh, I thought you were here to annoy me," I teased. She threw a pillow at me.

"No, contrary to your antisocial ways, I'm actually here to do you a solid."

"Does it include vodka?"

"I don't like lush Baby," she pouted.

"Whatever, okay, spit it out. What are you doing for me?"

"You know we have another trial in a couple of hours?"

"Yeah, who's up on the chopping block?"

"The leader, Junior, it's going to be a circus."

"You gotta go to this one?" I asked, thinking about yesterday's craziness.

"No, well, yeah. I could say something, but I have a feeling my interactions with Junior are nothing compared to what he did to other people. My testimony isn't going to be needed."

"That's gonna be a horror show," I shivered.

"It is. They also want to let some of the bikers get the chance to speak for him." She looked at me intensely.

"None of them will speak for him, unless it's positive."

"Positive, negative, we have to give them the chance to speak. Three have agreed to speak, we don't know what they will say. They want Rebel to speak, but he won't even talk to anyone."

"I guess he's tired of being used," I said without thinking.

"Is that what you think?"

"What else would you call it? He risked his life, sold out a group of men he's known since he was a kid, taught these fools how to get electricity up and running and then they have him locked in a box, waiting to be killed."

"I don't think they'll kill him," Lex said, but I could sense the doubt in her voice. There was no way to tell. Blake and Zach could be set on keeping him alive, but Ryan and Poche might be out for blood. And who knows how the civilians will vote. Who knows what people will say during the trial. Maybe he had participated in some of the behavior that was getting these bikers a guilty verdict. I didn't think so, but you never know.

"Then they'll exile him. Either way, it's a death sentence. Wonder if Clara is still kicking?" Lex flinched and I regretted my words. The bitch deserved her fate, but it was still a life. We were still killing people. Living, breathing people. People who weren't fighting back. This was nasty shit. Was it justice? At this point I couldn't tell. We might call it exile, but it was delaying the inevitable. Clara didn't have the life-skills to survive in this world. We should have put a bullet in her head, it would have been more humane.

"At least with exile they have a fighting chance. They exiled the guy this morning."

"What were his crimes?"

"The only people that spoke for him were civilian men. He liked to use his fists for emphasis. He was one of the lookouts, so he was never at the base and doesn't seem to be one of the addicts. You should hear the stories upstairs, half of the men are in withdrawal. Isaiah is giving them low doses of meth to keep them from going into shock."

"Nasty shit," I cursed.

"The trial starts in two hours, can you get Rebel?"

"So you want me to talk him into speaking for Junior?"

"Yes, you have two hours," she smiled. She thought she was doing me a favor. I had to talk this man into sitting through a trial, one he'll be forced to take center-stage on tomorrow. I have to ask him to speak for a man he grew up with, to give testimony that would probably aid in ending the man's life.

"I can't make any promises," I said curtly.

"I know you can't, Baby, if you only sit there for two hours with him, at least you tried. C'mon." She stood and held out her hand. "You might want to change though, that outfit is rank."

FIFTY-EIGHT

SENT IN THE BIG GUNS

REBEL

I couldn't stew anymore, so I had taken to sporadically jumping up and doing fifty push-ups. It wasn't making the time any more bearable but at least I wasn't drowning in self-pity.

The door handle jiggled and I shot up. If it was Poche's lackey, Graf, again, I was going to go off on him. He was one of the soldiers from the National Guard and he was acting as Poche's personal assistant or something. He had been in here three times on the premise of delivering my food, but he had ulterior motives. I was seriously done with this racket. He wanted me to sit through Junior's trial, thought it would be helpful if I spoke up about Junior's leadership. You know, from a person like me, it will hit harder. Quicker to kill him off.

Let the traitor dig his hole deeper and really put the nail in his brother's coffin was more like it.

I should have stayed in that apartment. I thought I was being altruistic or something like that. I thought I needed this. I thought I needed these people. I thought she'd never respect me if we ran...

"Rebel," her voice cut through me like a knife. I turned around and she stood there, in the doorway. The scent of lavender was in the air as if she had cleaned up before she came here. Her hair was loose and long down her back, something she had only done once in my presence. She was in a pair of black cargo pants and a tight tan tank under a leather jacket. She looked amazing.

"They've sent in the big guns," I said under my breath and her quiet regard confirmed she had been sent to bring me to the trial.

"I didn't make any promises. I'm just here, I'm here to talk." She closed the door and approached me.

Talk. Sure.

I was suddenly angry. I was pissed at the entire situation. At my choices, at what could have happened.

"What do you want to talk about, Baby?" I walked forward, making her step back. The office was small so she was up against the wall two steps later. I caged her in with my arms. I looked down at her and tried to be mad, but I couldn't.

She looked up at me defiantly. I had a foot on her, but she stared me down. This tiny thing had more fire in her than anyone I had ever met.

"How stupid you are," she shot back.

"Is that right?" I stepped back and pushed the hot flare of anger down.

"We could have fucking left," she hissed. "But you had to come back to this. I don't fucking get it."

"Being on my own is a death sentence," I said.

"I would have stayed with you," she said quietly.

"For how long? And could you have lived with yourself? Abandoning your friends? For what, me? Some washed up low-life who didn't have the balls to stand up for what was right?"

"Is that what you think of yourself?" she asked, pity in her eyes. I didn't want her to pity me. That look in her eyes ripped me apart, made me feel even more of a low-life.

"I know where I stand, and you shouldn't be here."

"I want to be here," she said.

"Why, you want more of this?" I moved quickly, caging her in again. It was a jerk move, but I pressed myself up against her. I might as well embrace my low-life status. She didn't push me away, instead her small hands pressed against my chest and she looked up at me with those damn blue eyes.

"It's what I'm really good at." I whispered and I took her mouth, sucking her bottom lip into my mouth and nibbling on it.

She moaned against my lips and my consciousness narrowed to that moment. I was starved for her. I wanted every part of her. I needed to touch and taste, but most of all I needed to be inside of her. She pulled at me and I pushed back. I yanked her jacket off her shoulders and threw it on the floor.

She kicked out; the thump of her boots on the floor a wonderful sound. I pulled her tank up, she was braless.

Lucky for me, my little cell had wall to wall glass windows on the back wall. I could see clearly with the light that came through- her body, her skin, the flush of her excitement. She was perfection. She was always perfection. Her nipples were hard and erect. I sucked one into my mouth and she arched against me as her hands went to my hair.

She squirmed, kicking off her pants until she was completely nude and under my control. I hadn't removed a stitch of clothing. I unbuckled my pants and released my cock. I was hard and ready. I pulled her to me and she wrapped her legs around my waist as I found her wet and ready center and I slid inside. Perfection. She took every inch of me and moaned my name as I seated myself in her core.

"Reid," she sighed as I began to pump into her. I kept her braced against the wall and with each thrust I drew a small moan from her. Holding her up and keeping a steady pace wasn't easy, but I tried my damnedest. When she came, she came hard but quietly. She shook in my arms and I continued to thrust as she held on.

I had never felt so alive.

FIFTY-NINE

TYPICAL MALE

BABY

A second orgasm ripped through me and I would have sold my soul to keep this man around for more. He thought he was punishing me, he thought this was about teaching me a lesson. *I would take this lesson any day.*

He let me drop and I slid down the wall. I wanted him back inside me. I had never wanted anything more. Until he kissed me again. Then all I wanted was the kiss. I was caught in the moment. Focused down to one moment as time slowed and everything blurred out of existence. There was just him. Only him. He kissed me with such assertiveness, such hunger, I was unsteady on my feet when he finally let go.

"On the cot," he said gruffly and I shuffled over to the cot. I was about to lay down on my back when he barked out, "No." He pushed me down on my hands and knees.

Oh fuck.

He gripped my hips and slammed into me without prejudice. I saw stars and my body exploded in warmth. There was some weird keening sound coming out of my mouth. I tried to stop, but I couldn't help it.

My focus was completely skewed. I didn't know what was up and what was down. All I knew was Reid had me, I was his and I didn't want this to end.

It lasted for what seemed like hours, but ended in mere minutes. Too soon, the pleasure erupted and I froze, my orgasm so intense my vision blacked out. It pushed him over the edge and he came hard, holding onto my hips as he emptied inside of me.

He withdrew and I whined. I didn't want it to end. I heard him kick off his pants and he fell on the cot next to me. His chest rose and fell fast as he cooled down. I wrapped around his side, sad to see his beautiful cock not erect and ready. I gave him a few minutes of silence. His breathing became steady as his heart rate lowered and his body chilled in the un-heated room.

I began to stroke his dick. It was still wet with my juices and moved easily in my hand. He was eager and soon he was hardening in my hand.

"Hannah," he moaned as his dick lengthened and hardened more. "What are you trying to do? Kill me?"

When it was ready, I threw my leg over him and lined myself up with his body, I sat back and took him inside of me with a sigh.

I rode him. Up and down I moved my body over him. I leaned forward and he suckled my tits like he was starved for them. He grabbed my ass and tried to control the pace, but I pushed him off and rode him at the pace I wanted. When he stroked my clit, he rubbed me in the right place and pattern. I leaned back and completely abandoned myself to the pleasure.

We came together this time. The intense sensation was almost too much to handle. Blood pumped loudly in my ears, my heart beat insanely fast. I fell against his chest and he wrapped his hands around me, our bodies sticky with sweat and come.

He murmured something inaudible and when I turned my face to his, I heard it.

"I'm sorry."

Typical male.

SIXTY

WE'RE ALL FUCKED

REBEL

I didn't want her to leave. The sun shone over us as we lay on the cot and I felt at ease again. All the stress and worry faded away, drowned under the passion I had just experienced. I knew I had things that loomed over me, terrible things, but they didn't seem real now. All that felt real was her.

"What are you sorry for, Reid?" she asked, sitting up and looking down at me.

"I'm sorry I can't be the guy you deserve," I said in a low voice.

"I don't deserve a guy." She ran her hand over my chest. "I'm not the perfect female you think I am. You beat yourself up for what you didn't do. And you'll have to live with that, you'll have to live with the fact that you didn't act when you might have, that you followed the wrong people, one of which was your father. I'm following orders too, and I have to live with what I've done, the bad orders I've followed. You didn't act because it's not in your nature. You're not the type of person to pick up a weapon, I am. It doesn't make me more deserving, I'm just as fucked up. Probably more."

"You're not fucked up. You're amazing." I pulled her down and kissed her, not for sex, even though I felt my dick stir with her nearness.

"You're not so bad yourself," she whispered back.

"So, where does that put us?" I hated to ask. It's not like we had a future. At least, I didn't. I should be grateful I had this, this moment.

There was a knock on the door.

"Baby, the trial starts in ten minutes," Alexis called from the other side of the door.

"She's been out there the whole time?" I asked, suddenly embarrassed. Not for myself, but for Hannah. I didn't want to compromise her in that way.

"Out in a second," Hannah called and looked at me. "Someone had to guard the door, in case you took advantage of me and escaped." She smiled, "You managed one of those."

"I feel like I did," I grimaced.

"Shut-up and enjoy it. So, are you going to the trial?"

I didn't want to leave her, but if my days were numbered, if my fate was to be exiled or worse…I didn't want to waste any more hours. If that meant I had to watch Junior being flayed, so be it.

"Yeah, I'm going."

"Well, you better put some pants on, that might be a bit distracting." She motioned toward my dick and laughed.

"I think you need to take your own advice, Baby." She frowned and began looking around for her pants.

The place was packed. Someone had rounded up every chair they could find and put them in neat rows facing a folding table. Most of the women were present, along with a good portion of the civilian men. I even spotted a few of the brothers, Jazz, Midnight and Shakes, sitting off to the side under guard. They gaped at me when I walked in with Hannah at my side and took a seat near Alexis.

Hannah slipped her hand into mine and I watched as Alexis looked between the two of us, her face stoic, not judging, evaluating.

"Brandon Chambray, street name Junior, you've been accused of several crimes and have been brought in front of us to be tried for those crimes."

They led him out, his wrists still tied in front of him, and sat him in a chair facing the far wall.

Zach, Blake, Poche and three others I didn't know sat behind the table and stared at the man who had caused so much trouble.

"You've been accused of human trafficking, murder, rape, slavery and treason. Once we, the judges, come to a verdict, your sentence will be immediately carried out. Do you understand?" Zach finished.

"Fuck you," Junior spit, he didn't get a good arc on his cob so the remnants hung from his chin disgustingly. He jerked his head and wiped it on his tee while glaring at the audience. His eyes found mine and he smiled big.

Junior was a lunatic. There was no denying it now.

"If anyone in the audience would like to speak for Brandon Chambray, this is your time," Zach prompted the crowd.

No one did a thing. Everyone held as still as possible and Junior's smile grew wider. You could have heard a pin drop. They were still afraid of him.

Seconds ticked and the wait became unbearable. No one wanted to face this man.

I stood up.

"My name is Reid Gauthier, *street name* Rebel. I was initiated in the MC when I was eighteen. I'm legacy, my father and my grandfather were all members of the club. I grew up in the club and I'm the same age as Brandon, my father the Sergeant at Arms to his father. We were raised as brothers." I took a deep breath.

"When I was eight years old, Brandon took a hammer and killed a dog I found, because it was mine and he didn't have one. When I was twelve, he held me under the water in the pool because he wanted to 'see what it looked like when someone drowns.' He only stopped because my father came home. When I was seventeen, he had four of my brothers beat the crap out of me, broke both of my arms and four ribs, because I had been accepted into college. I was in the hospital for weeks. And this was all before the world ended, and I'm sure these things are only minor compared to other things that were done to his later victims. People that weren't protected by a father with clout. But, I thought I should give you an idea of what kind of man Junior is." I sat down and Hannah slipped her hand back into mine.

Junior glared at me. He mouthed the word 'pussy' and made some bizarre motion with his tongue. I shook my head and looked over, distracted by someone else standing to speak for him.

"My name is Kristy Ellis. Me and my mother came to this camp when our neighborhood was evacuated." I remembered Kristy's mother, she had been an attractive older lady who the brothers had called the cougar cunt.

"Junior said he liked my mother because she was old enough to know how to 'take it.' He raped her repeatedly and thought it was fun to give her meth. He also thought it was fun if he made me watch. He told me he'd never," her voice quavered, "fucked a mom and daughter at the same time before. So, I was a first."

Tears streamed down her face. The woman sitting next to her stood and put an arm around her. I could see both of them shaking from here.

"He liked to use stuff. He called them toys. They weren't like real sex toys, it was stuff. Just stuff he found. After a week of being used by Junior, my mother overdosed. I think she did it on purpose, but it was him, he killed her." Her chin jutted out and she stared at Junior who smiled back at her with glee. She sat down. Another woman stood up. And then another.

My whole body was shaking with fury as each one recounted horror after horror.

"He bought me from my stepfather, he said he would take care of me…"

"He killed my father and took me when he found us in a house only a few blocks from here…"

"…He liked to make us snort meth and he would do this thing with his gun…"

I looked at the crowd, tears were streaming down faces, some of the men looked ready to jump up and shoot Junior right there. Alexis was outright sobbing.

Baby was the only one with dry cheeks. I looked down at her and she glanced up at me. She wiped something off my face. Her fingers came back wet. I hadn't even known I was leaking.

"I'm so sorry," she mouthed and squeezed my hand.

I shook my head and we both looked to the side of the room as the first one of my brothers stood to tell their story. If he was about to defend him, I would walk out.

It was Jazz.

"My name is Lane Galvez, street name Jazz. I've killed five people for Junior." The room went silent, enraptured.

"The first one when I was only fourteen. He had me kill one of our friends who had disrespected us. Once I did that, I was his. I couldn't do anything without him holding that over my head and threatening to turn me in. The second one was his girlfriend. She made it through the biters, but he didn't think she should be in the 'new world.' We went to her house and set it on fire with her in it. The third and fourth were the officers in charge of this base, I can't even remember their names." He shook his head and shrugged. He was trying to stay hard, stay strong. I could see it in how he was holding himself, but his hand was fisted to control the shaking. He knew he was signing his own death certificate. I could see it in his face.

"Brandon and his father wanted control, so we snuck in while they slept and slit their throats. The fifth one was our brother, Tag."

Midnight and Shakes surged to their feet. One of their chairs got knocked over and flew back, hitting a soldier that stood on guard behind them. The soldiers grabbed the two men and held them back. Junior had told us that Tag was bit on a run. A run with him and Jazz. Tag was known for voicing his opinion too loudly. I had suspected something like that had happened.

"You didn't disobey Brandon, it didn't happen. If you did, you ended up dead. I'm not making excuses, I did what I did. He told me, I did it. Not anymore, this is the first thing I'm doing that no one told me to do." Jazz sat down.

Midnight and Shakes were known to be supporters of both the Brandons. I suspected they were here to talk him up. But, I had thought the same of Jazz. They were being restrained by the soldiers, but weren't putting up much of a fight.

"Do you have anything to add, gentleman?" Poche asked them.

"Nothing," Midnight growled, staring defiantly at Junior. Midnight had been good friends with Tag.

"Does anyone else want to speak for the accused?" Blake asked the crowd. No one said anything, enough was said.

"We'll have a verdict soon." Poche stood and the judges followed him from the room. Two minutes later, they filed back in with grim expressions.

"Junior, you are found guilty. We sentence you to death by firing squad. Your sentence is to be enacted immediately. Take him out," Poche said and three soldiers led him out while he screamed his head off.

"I'll see all of you in Hell!" It was the first time I wished there was a hell.

SIXTY-ONE

ANOTHER GUARD

BABY

I made it through that horrible trial without shedding a tear. Alexis had sobbed next to me, and even Rebel couldn't hold it back after we heard story after story of how much of a sociopath Brandon Junior was.

The tears didn't start until I started walking up the stairs to bring Reid to his cell. It was nothing too obvious, but I felt one or two salty drops leak down my face and roll off my chin. I was walking behind everyone, so no one saw me, hopefully.

I didn't care anymore, though. Reid was nothing like those men. Nothing. They would find that out tomorrow. *They had to.*

I grabbed him and threw my arms around him as one of the soldiers waited nearby to escort him inside his cell. He tried to pull away, but I held on. I kissed him and he gave in. He wrapped his arms around me and held on tight.

"We'll get through this," I whispered. "I'll make sure of it."

"Don't do anything stupid," he whispered back.

"But, that's the plan," I smiled up at him.

"Please, promise me, don't do anything that will compromise yourself. Promise." He looked at me earnestly, his eyes pleading.

"Have a little faith in me." I grabbed him by his cheeks and pulled him down to me and kissed him one more time as the soldier at the door cleared his throat.

I pulled away and watched with watery eyes as he walked into the room and the soldier closed the door behind him.

"Did a little more than get solar panels on your mission, Baby," the soldier smirked.

It felt so good when my fist made contact with his face. Even better when he hit the floor.

"You'll need another guard on this door," I called as I walked into the main lobby. Alexis followed me out of the room and tried to restrain herself. It didn't work, the moment we crossed the threshold she collapsed in a fit of laughter. I managed to hold back mine.

SIXTY-TWO

ESCAPE

BABY

We walked out of the main building into the yard, on a mission to keep ourselves busy, some how. There was a commotion from the West side of the yard and we stopped in our tracks as Zach rushed over to us with a pissed look on his face.

"He escaped!" he hollered.

"What do you mean, he escaped?" Alexis asked.

"Junior. He was helped by a civilian, they took out the soldiers. They left them dead, in the back lot. He's got at least an hour's lead time on us."

"Shit," I cursed. "Of all the people to get out. Why the hell didn't we find out earlier?"

"I have no idea," he said.

"Are we going after him?" Alexis asked.

"We aren't, he's not worth it. He'll go to ground. We would have to search every house in a five mile radius to find him. He's a lunatic, but he's smart. I sent out some of Poche's men to try and track him, but I know it's a lost cause."

"So, we give up, let him go? He's a maniac. He won't stop here, he'll do this again and again. He'll probably come back here for revenge." Alexis's face was flushed and she was breathing heavily.

"Alexis." Zach pulled her close. "He's on his own. He doesn't have his men. He won't be able to do anything. We can't risk our lives for his. He didn't die, but he is exiled. That's gotta be something."

"I don't like it," I said, looking at the couple. "I don't like someone out there like him."

"We don't have much of a choice," Zach said. "There's nothing we can do."

SIXTY-THREE

IS THIS A DREAM?

BABY

I slept terribly. My night was racked with the worst dreams. In one, I was trapped under water, something pulled at my feet. I was weighed down by my heavy boots and clothing. I awoke with a scream stuck in my throat. It was a common nightmare I had when I was stressed out, blame swim qualifications in Ranger school.

There was excitement in the hall, the noise had woken me.

"What the hell?" I got off my cot and poked my head out of the little cubby I was assigned to.

There were a few people running toward the stairs to the second floor. I followed out of curiosity, hoping it had nothing to do with a certain traitorous biker who was holed up there. Or a fugitive biker who had escaped today.

A large group of soldiers and troopers were congregating in the main area. I spotted Romeo and walked over to him.

"What's going on?"

"The radios are working. They got the tower up last night and the solar is working now. It was nothing but static all today, but they heard something."

"Come back, this is the 199th, out of New Orleans," a soldier sat at the com system and spoke into the microphone.

"199th, holy shit, I mean, come in 199th," a tinny voice said over the radio.

"199th here, identify yourself," the soldier said.

"199th, this is Fort Polk, glad to hear you're back in the game."

The entire room erupted in cheers and laughter. People were hugging each other, and a few of the tough guys and girls were caught wiping at their cheeks, embarrassed.

First contact.

There was no going back to bed after that. I knew I would only toss and turn. I was worried about Rebel. I was worried about him being exiled. And now if he was, he would be out there with that sociopath. *Exile was certain death.* I couldn't think about that.

It was close to six in the morning, so it wasn't that tough to stay awake. Reid's trial would start in a few hours. Everyone around me was buzzed with excitement about making contact with the large base in Central Louisiana. Conversation continued between our base and Fort Polk, mostly logistics. They wanted to know what kind of operation we were running.

Fort Polk was now a hub for the Gulf South and housed two senators from Texas and the Lieutenant Governor of Louisiana, who was now technically the governor since the Governor hadn't been heard from since it all went down. Polk was also in contact with the Capitol, which was now in rural Texas, since the president, who was still alive, had been on a visit down there when shit hit the fan.

We learned all this in five minutes. Our world expanded and became a national landscape again.

I sat there and listened to it for as long as I could. It was surreal. A President of the United States? A governor? Those terms seemed so outdated, so vintage. I couldn't process them. It was only a word. I wouldn't believe it until I could see it. Until I could walk out from behind high walls and feel safe.

I didn't think that was anytime soon. I noticed the guard from Reid's door had joined the madness, so I slowly slipped away. Romeo noticed where I was going and shook his head, but smiled. He too had heard the rumors, obviously.

I slipped into Reid's room and onto his cot. He didn't flinch as I gently woke him.

"Is this a dream?" he mumbled, but he was too aware of me to be asleep, the faker. He was also too ready as his body covered mine. His mouth trailed a lazy pattern down my neck.

I sighed with contentment as I felt his hand at my waistband.

"Yes," I moaned.

SIXTY-FOUR

IT'S ALL OVER NOW

REBEL

She slipped out right before it was time for my trial. Hopefully no one noticed her. She said she would be fine, no one was paying attention to this room. Something about the radio working now and getting in contact with a base up in Central Louisiana.

I got dressed and sat on the edge of my cot to wait it out. It was only a few minutes before there was a knock on my door and Graf came to collect me.

"I'm not going to restrain you, don't make me regret it," he said gruffly. I didn't deign to answer him. I had been nothing but compliant this entire time, his stupid words were only said to reinforce his dominance.

He led me downstairs and across the open yard. The day was warm, truly warm, not a chill in the air at all. The sky was a beautiful shade of blue and I could go without a jacket and only do shirtsleeves. It felt like it was over seventy degrees. It was one of those days when before the world went to hell, I would have gotten on my bike and driven out of the city just to get on the road and feel the warm air on my skin.

I looked up at the sun and blinked from the brightness. My gaze was drawn to the corner of the lot where a few of the biters pushed against the fence.

"You better take care of that," I said. "They build up, they'll push the fence down."

The fence wobbled under their onslaught. It wasn't reinforced, they needed to do something about that too.

"You need to worry about your own stuff," Graf responded and led me to the far building that used to be a drug store.

The room was nowhere near as packed as it was for Junior's trial. Hannah was in the front row next to a stoic Alexis and the guy people called Romeo. Felicity was in the second row, sitting with a woman I assumed was her mother. They looked similar. Her hair was still shorn tight to her head and I regretted doing that to her, since it wasn't necessary. *Bad timing as usual.*

Jazz was back and a few other women, including one I recognized. I winced, she wouldn't have anything good to say about me. I remembered what she had gone through and it wasn't pretty.

I was seated as the guest of honor and the judges filed in.

"Reid Gauthier, street name Rebel, you've been charged as an accessory to a human trafficking ring, accessory to rape, accessory to murder and assisting known traitors to the United States of America," Poche said.

They were getting more formal now that they had made contact with the chain of command.

"Your actions will be judged by this panel. Once a verdict is given, we will sentence you immediately. Do you understand this?"

I nodded. *Yup. Got it.*

"We are asking for anyone in the crowd to stand up and speak for the accused."

It didn't take long. A woman in the back stood up. I recognized her as being the woman Eagle had claimed.

"I'm Sarah Lake, I was considered Eagle's property. Rebel escorted me to Eagle who was organizing the stores, or something. They didn't tell us anything, so I don't know what he was doing, really. The only thing I knew was that he liked to rape me. Eagle, not Rebel," she stuttered and I felt terrible for her. I knew what Eagle was capable of.

"But, Rebel," she went on, "He took me off base and brought me to one of the houses, because Eagle requested me. He could have let me go, but he delivered me to that sadistic bastard. I asked him to let me go, but he didn't." She sat back down gruffly and I frowned at her statement.

I had done that. *Guilty.* No excuse.

Felicity's mother stood up. I braced for impact.

"I'm Vivian Barrow, this is my niece, Felicity Barrow," she motioned for Felicity to stand up and ran a hand over the girl's shaved head. "She's only fourteen. We were reunited after you took over the base and I was shocked to see her dressed like a boy with her head shaved. When I asked her what had happened, she told me Rebel made her do it. My first thought was that he was some kind of pedophile and liked little boys or something."

Ouch. I shook my head, I didn't like where this was going. I was screwed. *Fucked.*

"But she told me the story, about how a man had come in and gave her too much attention. Rebel had told her this was a bad place to be pretty and he had made some of the boys shave her head and give her boy clothes to wear. This isn't a world for pretty girls, was what she said. He saved my niece from my fate. I will be forever grateful to him."

I had been sitting forward in my chair and I sat back with a whoosh of air. Stunned.

The aunt sat back down and the woman I was worried about stood up. This was all going so fast. I wanted it to slow down, to delay the inevitable. I looked over at Hannah, our eyes met. She stared at me, nothing but compassion and feeling in her eyes. Our gazes remained locked. And suddenly the stress of this ordeal faded from me. If she could look at me this way, everything would be okay.

"I'm Tina, I testified at Eagle's trial. I was his property too, Eagle's, not Rebel's. Rebel was actually the one that brought me in, to the base." Everyone kind of gasped as one. It was what I was afraid of. Not an accessory. Talk about regret.

"It was before the Brandons had killed the National Guardsman, I thought it was a good thing. I thought I was saved. I don't know if Rebel knew about what was going to happen. I can't tell you that. He told me I would be safe. I doubt Rebel knew what the bikers planned, though. Eagle always joked about Rebel, how he was – well, he liked to call him names a lot. I never blamed Rebel. I just wanted to say that, I never blamed him. He said it was safe and it was. I would have died out there alone. I lived. I'm alive. It was rough going at first, but I'm alive and that is all that matters."

She sat down and a girl next to her hugged her. I was in shock. I broke my gaze with Hannah and looked over at the woman who had given me too much credit. Sure, I hadn't known Senior would start forcing the women to have sex, but I should have. I should have known what they planned. I was one of them. But she had spoken for me. I suddenly felt lighter. *I had a chance.*

I was still in shock when Melinda stood up.

"My name is Melinda Lemoine. I was at this base from the very beginning. I don't even know what it's like out there. But, I know what it's like in here. I know that to pay for a night with a girl, the bikers used to accumulate food credits. This was earned by doing certain undesirable chores, or going on food runs and bringing back supplies. One of the biggest ways to earn food creds was by being a scout or lookout. Rebel was both, he had a lot of food creds. When he wasn't on lookout, he liked to use his food creds on me." Again, a gasp from the crowd. But I knew what was coming. Melinda wouldn't let me down.

"He had a sleeping bag in his cubby and he let me sleep on his cot, while he slept on the floor. He never touched me, he hardly even talked to me. Said he didn't want to make me feel obligated to like him," she laughed. "He saved me because Spider had voiced his interest in me. That was all it took, and most of my nights were spent with him in relative safety. All because of one comment from that sadist. I owe my sanity to Rebel." She sat down, but then stood up abruptly. "And yes, when he was sick with the flu, I wanted to sneak him out of this place. He doesn't deserve to be tried like the rest of these animals. He's a good person. If you want to look at me like I'm guilty too, so be it. You've got the wrong man up there."

Everyone sat in stunned silence, even me. I looked around at the crowd and everyone was regarding Melinda with respect, not suspicion.

No one stood up after that and everyone looked at each other. They were probably thinking, was this it? Nothing juicy. Nothing worth getting worked up about. *Would they give a judgment now? Was I guilty?*

Poche went to get to his feet when the screech of a chair on the linoleum had my head shooting up.

It was Hannah.

"Hey." She gave a wave of her hand. "Hannah Klink, street name Baby," she smirked and Alexis barked out a laugh. "Y'all might remember me, I was the one that helped you get this base back from the *evil* bikers." That smirk again.

"I was the one that brought Rebel in. He was protecting the children when I found him and he came in without a fight, he even wanted to help when he found out we were with the military." She put her hands on her hips and glared at the judges.

"I was also the one that risked life and limb, *with Rebel*, lost a good friend, almost died, all to get you power. I might add that when we lost Murphey, Rebel was right there. He saved my life. Got me to safety and made sure we still finished the mission. Then he came back here and taught y'all how to install the equipment. To bring electricity to this place. Without him, you wouldn't have gotten in contact with Fort Polk. Oh, and then you stuck him in a cell and then put him on trial for human trafficking. Does that about cover it?"

The judges were staring at her like she was insane. I could have gotten up right there and kissed her. She was amazing.

"And yeah– one more thing. I'm pretty sure I'm in love with him, so if you exile him, or worse– consider me gone too."

SIXTY-FIVE

MORE CONVICTION

BABY

My speech worked. They didn't spend thirty-seconds locked away behind closed doors before they came back and said simply, "Not guilty." It was Zach who announced it and he smiled at me as he said it.

"I'm pretty sure we would have voted not guilty without you shaming us," Zach said as he patted Rebel on the back as if they were old friends. I glared at him.

"Then why the charade?" I asked.

"It wasn't a charade. We said before we knew about Rebel that we would try all of the Southern Clan members. If we went back on it for any reason, others could get out of it for this reason or that. We didn't want to give any reason for someone to call into question our judgment. We plan on doing things like this from now on. If we go back on our word in the first pursuit of justice, what precedent would that set?" He said it earnestly. And he was right.

"We also would like to invite you to join our group," Blake added as he walked up to us. "We could use someone with your talents and well, Baby, she's indispensable," he laughed.

"Where she goes, I go," Rebel said and he caught my eye. "Just, are we leaving anytime soon?"

"No, we still have a few more trials and then we'll head back," Blake said.

"Good, so I can go back to my cell?"

"You – you're free to do whatever you want, Rebel," Blake said confused. "Why would you want to go back to your cell?"

"It's got four walls and a door, better than anything y'all got." He looked at me and winked. I shook my head and smiled.

"Yeah," Blake laughed and looked at Zach like they could relate. "It's all yours."

"Thanks," Rebel said as he dragged me away.

"So, you think you love me?" he asked when we got to the stairs. He hadn't let go of my hand.

"Something like that," I replied.

"Not a very assertive statement. You would think if you were going to declare your love for someone in front of a crowd of people, you would do it with a little more conviction." He turned to me as we got to the second floor, a smile on his face.

"I didn't want to scare you off," I smiled back.

"Nothing you can do will scare me off, Hannah Klink, street name, Baby. I've been in love with you since you told me to put my hands up and called me a fuck face." He pulled me to him and brought me to my knees with one of those leg-shaker kisses.

I came up for air and realized we were in the middle of the lobby which was being used as the communication room. Everyone was staring.

"Now, you have to admit, that's how you do it," he chuckled, grabbed my hand and pulled me into his cell.

ABOUT THE AUTHOR

Gillian Zane is the author of the NOLA Zombie series. Zane is the pen name of a prominent blogger in the publishing industry, which will remain a mystery unless you Google it. Since she can remember her goal has been to become Master of the Universe and she has decided to focus first on the literary world. Things are progressing nicely.

Zane has been a freelance writer for the last ten years and has published a few non-fiction works, none of which were very exciting. Zombies are much more exciting and a way for her to combine her two current obsessions, hot boys with guns and Doomsday Prepping. When she isn't stockpiling MREs or researching how to build a cistern on a budget, she's taking care of her little family and exploring the city that she loves, New Orleans.

Follow Gillian on Twitter: @GillianZane

www.ingramcontent.com/pod-product-compliance
Lightning Source LLC
Chambersburg PA
CBHW070857180626
46817CB00003B/811